Murder, Mustard and Cheese

On a quiet October afternoon in the village where Peggy Pinch is the policeman's wife, an old lady is poisoned in her parlour armchair.

It is 1931 and folk with murder in their midst seem more concerned about Ogden's unfair circulation of cigarette cards and the fate of Hedley's Fairy Soap. Some newcomers are finding village life difficult while senior housewives in the Red Lion's snug are resolute in their guardianship of parish morals. Peggy cannot solve this murder without discovering the truth behind the myth that a German spy is living amongst them. No more than village gossip? Or did this traitor have a hand in the killing of Spinster Knightly?

As a young man Malcolm Noble served in the Portsmouth police. He has written sixteen mystery novels set in the south of England from the 1920s to the 1960s. Press reviews have emphasised his sense of place and atmosphere, his strong characterisation and first rate storytelling. He is a member of the Crime Writers Association.

'This is Parochial Policing at its Best' says the *Shropshire Star*

Malcolm Noble's Crime Fiction

"The books feature a host of interesting and unusual characters as well as a well defined sense of time and place."
(John Martin/Crime Scene Britain and Ireland: A Reader's Guide)

"Good fun and a fast enjoyable read."
(Shropshire Star)

"Noble has a fine knack of description, creating a sense of place and atmosphere. Try them."
(Portsmouth Post)

"A dead good read. A mesmerising murder mystery."
(Harborough Mail)

"Suspenseful, darkly funny and beautifully written."
(Historical Novels Society)

"A great success. Very talented writing skills."
(102.3 Harboroughfm)

"A marvellous creation. Noble reels off a first rate story. Vastly entertaining. Noble makes good use of his knowledge of the world of crime."

(Nottingham Post)

"An original, absorbing and compulsive read for all fans of this genre."

(Telford and Wrekin Advertiser)

"This fantastic new novel. It leaves you begging for the next in the series."

(Montgomeryshire Advertiser)

"This is parochial policing at its best."

(Shropshire Star)

"If you like your murder mysteries, these books are for you."

(BBC Leics)

"The books show a humorous and tongue-in-cheek view of village life in times gone by."

(Eats, Reads and Dream Cookbook)

by the same author

Peggy Pinch Investigates
Peggy Pinch, Policeman's Wife
Murder in a Parish Chest
The Body in the Bicycle Shed

"Parochial Policing at its Best" *(Shropshire Star)*
malcolmnoble.com

Malcolm Noble

Murder, Mustard and Cheese

featuring
Peggy Pinch, the Policeman's Wife

Bookcabin Press
Market Harborough
2023

Selected for The Crime Stock

First published at the Bookcabin
Leicestershire

Murder, Mustard and Cheese

FIRST EDITION

1

140.216.103

ISBN 978-1-9998092-7-0

Cover image by Oberholster Venita from Pixabay
Page iv photo by John Heywood
Back cover photo by Christine Noble

For Christine

Peggy Pinch's Village

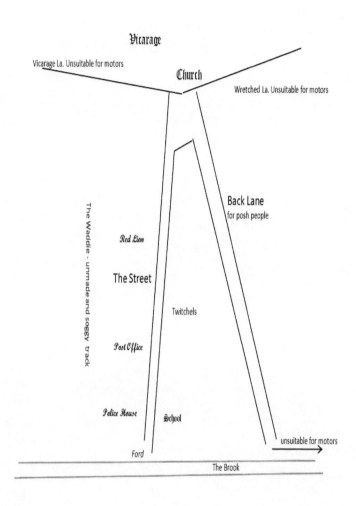

Vicarage

Vicarage La. Unsuitable for motors

Church

Wretched La. Unsuitable for motors

Back Lane
for posh people

The Waddle - unmade and soggy track

Red Lion

The Street

Twitchels

Post Office

Police House

School

unsuitable for motors

Ford

The Brook

A Village Directory

Eliza Knightly, the dead body.

Arthur Pinch, the village policeman.
Peggy Pinch, the policeman's wife.

Rev. Sullivan, the new vicar.
Polly Adam, the new vicar's help.

Farmer Wistow, a yeoman.
Jacoby, the new gamekeeper.

William Wheeler, a bank clerk.
Tommy Wheeler, his son.

Dr Ernest Meriweather, the village doctor.

Mavis Reynolds.
Miss Maud Nevers.
Julie Cart (of Cart and Gort)
Irene Gort (of Cart and Gort)
Poppy Anders of Laurel Cottage.
Dolly Johnson of Little Firs.

George Templar, a solicitor.
Lettice Templar, a solicitor's wife.
Deborah Twinn, a solicitor's mistress.

Sir Roland of Byrivers Hall.

and others as may be revealed

Chapter One

The Sad Passing of Spinster Knightly

For as long as Police Constable Arthur Pinch had been completing his bicycle patrol of the parish, strictly an after lunch routine, Peggy Pinch had been kneeling on a remnant of stair-carpet and tugging at the weeds beneath their hedge bottom. She bent forward so that her bottom faced whatever was going on in The Street, but her old coat, long tailed and chocked with patches, and her generous tweed skirt made sure that no passers-by could share her rear end impertinence. Still, doing it well tickled Peggy Pinch.

She could hear Edna Carstairs, Peggy's old schoolma'am, creating a commotion as she cleared her apple shed with clatters and bangs that enticed the shrill children on their afternoon playtime next door. Further up The Street, Julie Cart and Irene Gort (informally, Cart and Gort) had been gossiping for so long outside the Post Office, closed until four, that they must surely be ready for their pot of afternoon tea and buttered dough biscuits. Across the road from the post box, neighbours Mavis Reynolds and Maud Nevers weren't on speaking terms. Each made sufficient noise in their gardens that the other had more than an excuse to engage over the fence but, so far, there was no meeting of minds. Doctor Meriweather and the vicar, both new to the village, had been with Poppy Anders for five and twenty minutes; Dolly Johnson had been at her staircase window for just as long but could make no sense of what was going on in

Poppy's Laurel Cottage, though she was well on the way to making things up. At half past three, by the chime of the church tower clock, Farmer Wistow, bendy willow in hand, guided three messy cows from the bottom of The Street to the top.

"Good day, Mrs. Pinch."

"Good afternoon, farmer," said Peggy, face down. (She had wanted it to sound like a Catholic 'father'; she wasn't sure that Wistow got the joke.)

In a little shed in the back garden of the Red Lion, Jamie Eider was playing truant. He wanted to be a scientist. Truthfully, he had learned little from his Chem Craft chemistry set, although he had made all the right noises on his birthday morning. He knew that these presents weren't cheap. Most of Jamie's discoveries had been the product of his own investigation. He had learned how to extract sap from trees from which he had made a nicely scented polish that worked well on his scraps of wood. And he had invented a liquid for removing rust. He kept quiet about this because it had an unexplained propensity to catch fire. Fat from dead mice had helped his own cuts and sores heal quickly, and he was sure that Miss Reynold's home made mustard, rubbed in deep, made it easier to prick skin. This worked on cats as well as young boys but he needed to experiment on cows, if it was to be of any use. His different applications were lined up in irregular pots and jars on the shed's shelf. Jamie Eider knew that he had more brains than other children in the village; he wanted to visit a volcano one day.

Peggy, still working away, heard the crunch of gears as the village bus mastered the brow of Capstan Hill, perhaps a mile away, and commenced its free-wheel down the side of the valley.

In just a few minutes, the bus would splash through the shallow ford at the bottom of The Street. Known as The Bottom.

"Bottom!" Peggy cursed aloud as the truculent dock leaf refused to give. "Blinking bottoms!" And she stuck her rear end more deliberately in the face of the village and all its works.

Peggy Pinch, the policeman's wife, was discontented.

' 'Tis the cruellest month for knees.' Some of the words she chuntered, others stayed in her head. Who said that? Someone wrote it, she was sure. October is the cruellest month for dock leaves. 'They make widows of us all.' She was working on a troublesome root, waggling, levering and excavating like a dentist. She mumbled, "It won't even rhyme." Peggy's poems were supposed to rhyme but few did. Worse, this one made no sense. Widows? Try weaklings. Or better still, minnows. 'They make minnows of us all.'

"Blast!" She sat back on her heels. Something had got inside the ragged fingertips of Pinch's second best gardening gloves and stung her.

'I leave unto my wife my second best gardening gloves.' She took off the glove and made a noise, something like a French whisk trying to make its way through mashed potato, as she sucked on the inflamed finger. She was sure that the quotation was another famous snippet.

It was October 1931. Britain had left the gold standard, Ramsay MacDonald had formed a National Government and the country was falling headlong into a General Election which would return another Labour Government. European statesmen looked to Germany with increasing unease while Americans needed two years patience before FDR's fireside chats could take their place in the myth of the economic recovery.

An observer might have judged that Peggy's sleepy English village was more concerned about the prospects for Horace Wistow's flock of Southdown sheep at a forthcoming Gloucestershire show, or the noisy performance of a Spider racing car on a Worcestershire hillside. This automotive replica of a nineteen-twenties original had been built in a garden shed on Back Lane and as many lobbied for its name to be painted on a sign at the end of the 'No Through Road' as damned it for its noisy nuisance. People suspected that Ogden cigarettes were withholding a picture of the Spider until the very last weeks of their 'faggies' featuring Motor Races of 1931. Some said that the first village smoker to find the card should donate it to a pool so that lots could be drawn. Peggy couldn't see that happening. Mary in the Post Office had come under fire. She had been unable to stock Hedley's candles when larger shops in town still had supplies. But they were carrying old stock, she insisted and even displayed the latest copy of the Grocer, announcing that the brand had been withdrawn. Mary promised that Fairy soap bars, from the same people, would carry on and, thank goodness, the rumours that Vim was vanishing had come to nothing, further debilitating Dolly's standing as a fountain of trusty news. Mavis Reynolds was the troublemaker who never accepted what she was told. She needed putting right, some said.

These topics rarely featured in conversations beyond the Post Office shop. In the pub and on the bus, over garden gates and coming out of church, recent chatter had complained about the raising of subs at the vestry whist drive and the absence of any decision over the maintenance of the ford. There was a campaign for a vigilante committee to take possession of the Twitchels, a wilderness area in the centre of their parochial world, so that volunteer labour could make something of this forgotten ground. Others whispered that the new vicar had come to the parish with controversy or scandal attached to his name. True insiders, a group of no more than five or six senior housewives of pensionable age, each with more than forty years memories of church affairs and who knew what was going on in the very intestines of village life, were busy with an idea - not even talk at this stage - of a woman carrying the child of someone else's husband. But another three formidable women, known as the Snuggery, wanted to know the authority for such gossip? Without the detail, 'keep quiet,' they said and got on with drinking their bottles of Robin Hood pale ale in the tinted room set aside from the public bar of the Red Lion.

In these ways, Peggy Pinch witnessed the careful regulation of common talk in the true traditions of the English village. The new vicar's maid, thought by many to be simple, was congratulated on her Autumn flowerbeds, just two weeks before Harvest Festival, yet she got short shrift when she asked about the legend of Byrivers Hall. And still, two people - each unaware of the other's suspicions - believed that for many years a German spy had lived deceitfully amongst them.

It began as a squawk, a child's response to something that hurt and something unfair. It gained little attention. It came from the top of The Street, so probably had little to do with Peggy or her neighbours lower down. Birds broke free of the church belfry and a brace of free range hens scuttled and clucked from the verges of the road.

Gort's dog barked.

Then the noise became a squeal in the middle of the lane, going out of control and beyond anyone's comprehension as a boy in short trousers and a hand-knitted waistcoat ran the length of the thoroughfare, his arms waving and his throat choked with tears. Cart and Gort tried to catch him as he raced past the Post Office, but they missed him.

While people at the bottom of the village wanted to gather the boy up and keep him safe, their neighbours at the top had identified Miss Knightly's quaint and fussy home as the root of the child's distress and wanted to know what might have happened in Wayback Cottage.

Wistow 'wo-hoed' his stock on the village green and, having by quirk of circumstance a lawful curiosity about the humble thatched cottage, ambled towards the rose-thorn covered gate. He held his willow stick afore, threatening serious business for any idle perpetrator. The old lady in Wayback Cottage had been a well loved soul.

Some people would recall that the child's wailing seemed peculiarly eerie. Some said that the echoes of his squawks came from the clouds, as if heaven herself was hurting, while those who believed in ghouls and ghosts and widows on broomsticks swore that the boy's yell was echoed by a witch's cat. The investigation would never be totally free of this supernatural texture.

So many people raced this way or the other that, later on, in the quiet of her evening's reflection, Peggy wouldn't be able to bring her memory to order. The ringing of Pinch's bicycle bell could be heard as he broke through the Twitchels of Back Lane. The doctor was stretching his stride, wanting to be quick but

16

determined not to run across The Street. Farmer Wistow was already treading his muddy Wellington boots on the lush carpets of the spinster's cottage, while Cart and Gort preferred to stand on a dead woman's flower bed and peer through the bow window of her parlour.

"Can't see anything. It's so dark. There's a big man."

"Likely, Mr Wistow. Is he moving about?"

"Oh, my God. She's lying in her armchair."

The bicycling policeman had his knees out and was wobbling. Still working the tinny sounding bell, he was soon alongside Meriweather but in no condition to talk. His clumsy working of the left hand brake slewed the rear wheel to the right. The heavy police boot slammed to the ground and the bike dropped between his trouser legs. With great dignity, he stepped away, before picking it up by one hand-grip. Rather like taking a child by its ear. Half a dozen villagers were clustered at the garden fence, making sure that the gate was kept open and the pathway clear.

Small Thin Annie wept that she didn't know what to do. "I always give her my coupons from Lipton packets." She curled a lock of her black hair around a worried finger.

Someone said, "We don't know that she's gone yet."

But the three messy cows knew. They stood quietly on the little triangle of grass, watched over by the church tower and the ugly turret on the vicarage attic. They sensed and respected death and accepted that this was no time for bovine misconduct. The mongrel, a vagrant who had been seen around the parish for three weeks, slunk quietly through the Twitchels to the sheltered spot between Maud Nevers back hedge and the abandoned hedge-watcher's billet. Queen O'Scots, the schoolma'am's cat, appeared on the flat roof of the police house shed. She too caught the scent of death, and she kept to herself all that she knew.

Then, incongruously, the bright blue racing car emerged from the top of The Street and, propelled by a series of back-blasts that were surely out of order, ran down to The Bottom without serviceable brakes. The stink of the exhaust smoke polluted every green garden and got through every crack in windows and doors. Immediately, grumbly grandpas and sickly children swore as to sore throats, and ladies, brought up to know better, dabbed clean handkerchiefs to their eyes. Someone called out, 'Who was that?' and, though many young boys answered 'The Spider', no one knew the driver's name.

High in the sky, a sparrow hawk circled, his screeches and aerobatics seemed to reflect the distress. He came low, tracing the high chimneys that reached up from the rectory, then swirled up again.

The attraction of a dead body in their midst meant that most of the villagers had lost interest in the young child. He had exhausted the hue and cry. He ran with his arms flaying and his weakening knees only just able to keep him on his feet. He was shouting, "Mrs. Pinch! Mrs. Pinch, catch me!"

Peggy Pinch stepped backwards into the middle of The Street, held her arms open and collected the shaking, panting and weak limbed boy to her scruffy bosom.

"Spinster Knightly's gone to our Maker." Tears seemed to flow from every fold in his face.

"Let's you and me go inside," she said warmly. "Everyone else can sort it out. Goodness me, you've raised a proper alarm."

At that moment, the bird of prey swept down to the rectory garden and settled on the outstretched sleeve of the new vicar's maid.

"Peacefully, at her home," said the doctor and withdrew from his patient. "There's nothing untoward, Pinch, as far as I can tell." He wore flannels and a sports jacket. His balding auburn hair had been combed and greased back from his forehead and he had rested his spectacles on his brow. Pinch didn't like the man.

Miss Eliza Knightly was at rest in the armchair at her hearth. There was no knitting, no cup of tea, no magazine and no letters. But her head was to one side and Pinch fancied just the hint of a smile, as if she were remembering something nice.

The doctor said, "I'd say, she's been dead for something short of an hour."

P.C. Pinch observed, "She was expecting someone." In the far corner, a tray of scones was waiting, untouched, on an occasional table. "A spoonful of mustard on a saucer."

"Nothing unusual in that," judged the doctor as he felt beneath her ears and the base of her skull.

"With cheese scones?" Portly Pinch observed, "Her feet seem twisted." He stepped back. His old fingers went reflexively to the tobacco pipe in his tunic pocket, but, no, this was no time to smoke. "It helps me take things in," he muttered to himself.

He wished that Meriweather would stop poking at her. (Pinch had known the good woman since the war.)

"Yes, I noticed that," said the doctor who hadn't heard the mutter. "I'd say that she was standing up when it happened, and she fell backwards into the chair." The doctor stood straight and

19

put his hands deep in his trouser pockets. "The mustard? Someone wanted to disguise the taste of cheap margarine, I should think." He inhaled deeply through his nose. "There's nothing for you here, Pinch. Really."

"You were treating her for something?"

"A failing heart. I cannot say that death is unexpected. I'll report to the Coroner at once; it shouldn't be a long job." The doctor sighed at the simplicity of someone's passing. He had always thought that a doctor should have more to do. "She made a will, I know that. In fact, Templars were supposed to be here, drawing up an inventory this afternoon."

"There's no family," Pinch said.

"Talk of a sister in London, but they haven't spoken in years. Some sort of scandal, I believe."

At that moment, the farmer reappeared at the parlour door. "No," he growled. He had checked each of the upstairs rooms. "Ah, no. There's no scandal. A family rift, as sure as day, but no scandal."

Peggy Pinch spread three sheets of newspaper across the breakfast table and lifted the young fellow so that she could, very lightly, assess the muddy knees.

"What do you think, Master Tommy? Could this be a kitchen sink job?"

He kept two fingers at his mouth and nodded.

"Then get yourself undressed while I do the water." She was about to say that he could keep his underpants on, but he had already untied the string around his shorts, revealing that he owned no underpants. The seat of his trousers were padded with a sheet of thick brown paper, unsoiled in spite of everything. Beneath the waistcoat and blouse, he wore a grown-up's vest which fell like a skirt to his knees. He had no hope of managing its huge arm holes.

Peggy sat him on the draining board, with his feet in the sink. "Now, then, a good scrub all over," she said, handing him a cake of coarse green Fairy soap, eight inches long and as thick as a doorstop, and a wire brush with which Mr Pinch had been known to scratch at rust. Peggy busied herself, first in the laundry passage, which led to the police house's only cell, and then in a cupboard beneath her staircase.

Tommy called through: "My aunty's been struck by lightning. That's why mummy's away."

Peggy wondered about that. Common talk hinted that times were difficult between his mother and father. She said, "Lightning? Goodness."

"My dad won't be home till eight and Spinster Knightly was keeping an eye on me."

Peggy returned to the kitchen. "Your clothes will be dry before morning. Meanwhile, you can put these on." She placed underpants, vest, blouse and socks on the wooden table; each had been carefully crafted and pressed by the welfare circle of village housewives.

"Dad won't do charity." He handled them as if their quality was beyond anything he had worn before. Peggy could tell that he wasn't used to underwear and, just for a moment, she wondered if he knew how to dress with them.

"Be sure, there's no charity," she said. "Every Police Station has a supply of clothes in case of civil emergencies. If we ever had a fire or a flood, people would need clothes to change into, wouldn't they? Now, what did you and Miss Knightly have for lunch?"

"Stewed apples with lashings of brown sugar."

"Lashings? My word."

"Not Miss Knightly, though. She was expecting someone for tea and had made some cheesy scones. Mrs. Pinch, can I put my bottom in? It's itching."

"Then we'll have more water. You do the cold."

He angled his body so that he could reach the single tap, while Peggy carried a saucepan of hot water from the stove.

"And after lunch?"

He smiled and dipped his head to one side where it enjoyed a happy memory. "She put me to bed for a sleep. She always did. The bedroom was always so spick and span and the blankets and eiderdown came up to my nose. I used to hear her listening on the landing but not this afternoon. This afternoon she felt too poorly and listened from the foot of the stairs."

"It must have been late when you woke up."

"I suppose. Sleeping's nice there. Sometimes I think I'm the luckiest boy alive because I've got two nice bedrooms that I love, one on each side of The Street. And people are always downstairs, talking or listening to the wireless or standing outside on the porch. But Spinster Knightly didn't feel well at all. She just sat in the armchair and panted. She was worried that Queen O'Scots was looking at her. I knew that it was nonsense and she was just imagining awful things, but we all know that Spinster Knightly was easily worried by things in the night. I know, it wasn't night time."

"I know what you mean."

"So I said I would go and find Queen O'Scots, then we'd know she was nowhere near."

"Did you see me weeding?" Peggy asked, still trying to get some sense of the timing.

"I went down the Waddie. I almost got to the Bottom but then I saw her on your shed roof. When I got back to Wayback Cottage, it was horrible. I couldn't wake her up. I'd never seen a dead one before but I could tell that she was. I should have been with her."

"Hey, come on, out you get. You'll catch your death sitting at my kitchen window in the nuddie." He stood up in the sink and she began to dry him vigorously with a roughish towel. Peggy explained, as gently as she could, "Some old people do like to send everyone away when they know that they are going to pass on. I remember sitting with my grandma for a night, a day and a night. Eventually, I had to pop to the privy in the garden and when I came back, she had slipped away."

"Elephants are the same," he dreamed, and said, very quietly, "I hope she knew that I was looking after her."

Peggy allowed herself to weep just a couple of tears. "Oh, I'm sure that's how it was. Tommy, you gave her one of her happiest days. In fact, I wouldn't be taken aback if the Almighty himself hadn't singled you out for the job."

Chapter Two

Evidence of a Footprint

By nine o'clock, Tommy Wheeler was asleep in his own bed, the doctor was in his surgery, sharing his third conversation with the Coroner (he was finding it difficult going) and Arthur Pinch was seated in his fireside armchair. He had taken off his shirt collar and unlaced his police boots. He drew his tobacco from a timber caddy of Bishop's Move; he knew no better flavour and he loved the tightly curled leaf, held together with the texture of sticky tar. On his lap: a volume of his favourite gardening literature. He was in no mood for Peggy to sit with him.

She noticed that he hadn't changed into his slippers, so he was thinking of patrolling The Street for a last time before lights-out. The villagers might be looking for that reassurance. For the same reason, he hadn't asked for his whiskey.

She ventured as far as the kitchen doorway. "Did Mister tell you any reason for Mrs. being away?"

Pinch, not wanting to encourage Peggy's curiosity, nibbled the tip of his pipe stem with two front teeth but did not reply. He knew that the sister had suffered a stroke. It had nothing to do with lightning.

She leant against the door-frame. "Pinch, we must take care of the lad."

"Because his ma and pa aren't wed?"

"There is that, of course, though I doubt young Tommy knows."

"He'll have heard." He hadn't lifted his face from the gardening book and spoke as if he wanted nothing to do with gossip.

"There's word that she's left him."

Pinch tutted loudly.

"Pinch, he loved Miss Knightly like his very own grandma. He loved her like I loved my own gran, for pity's sake. Now he's lost her and if he loses his mum or dad, he'll be devastated. He's such as sensitive little boy. Besides, it's all going to get more complicated."

Her husband wouldn't acknowledge that he was listening. He turned the page of the gardening book and lightly marked a margin with his pencil.

She persisted, "Mavis Reynolds called me in on Monday afternoon, after prayers."

"With news that Miss Nevers is expecting?"

"You know? How?"

"I don't know and neither do you." Keeping a thumb in his place, he closed the book and, with a nod, invited Peggy to sit in her armchair. "I was round the back of her place, two mornings ago, and caught sight of her at her kitchen sink, wrestling with the retching sickness. I made nothing of it. I said that I was worried about noises coming from her bottom hedgerow and was taking a look, that's all."

"Miss Nevers waits on one man and no other in our village. Willie Wheeler. She kept her crush a secret for months. But she tells Mavis everything eventually. You know what that pair are like."

"So, Mavis Reynolds thinks her friend is pregnant and Bill Wheeler is the father." He went back to his book. "It's village talk, Peg. That's all and we've let it keep us busy when we should have been listening to the nine o'clock news." He grumbled into his pipe. "Gone and missed it now."

"But if it is true, poor Tommy is the only soul that's going to get hurt." Sensing that her husband would not talk further of it and was close to going into a mood, she offered tentatively, "I thought I might take a run out to town tomorrow. I can take the Tuesday box to the station and pick up any packets from our dip."

Pinch sat still.

"Do you think we'll get a visit?"

He gave a sharp but faint shake of his head, hardly any movement at all. A Pinch who had missed the evening news was a Pinch out of sorts.

"The key ledger is checked and the petty cash. We've not had a soul in the cell for a twelve-month. The messages are all written up, but it's all in my handwriting, Arthur. Really, you ought to ..." She wanted to remind him how careful the couple needed to be but, no, this was not the moment.

He absorbed the criticism for a few seconds, then laced up his boots, stood in front of the mirror above the hearth and addressed his collar, before collecting his helmet from the bannister post in the lobby. He went without a word.

A down of clean white mist, icy cold but free of urban smoke and poisonous yellows, had lain across The Street and her front gardens. It turned the different lights of the cottages into peculiar lanterns. Truthfully, he was no less worried than his wife about their future, but while no one raised the subject, he would let the sleeping dog lie. The lamps in the houses looked like navigation lights likely to draw their vessels into collision.

Already, Miss Carstairs had allowed Queen O'Scots out for the night and the itincrant mongrel, with one leg limping, was going uphill where he would call on the charity of the vicarage. Pinch could hear the farmer working late in his barn; he was sure that if he walked to the top of The Street, he would catch the flickering lights of hanging paraffin lamps. He looked up at Tommy's bedroom; all quiet. Just three doors up from the police house, Dolly Johnson leaned forward on the garden gate of Little Firs. She wore a full petticoat with Border Anglaise at the shoulders and a cap which made Pinch think of an upturned embroidered purse. She liked to think that her dollopy breasts were spilling over the top of the gate.

"Laurel Cottage, Arthur. I'm keeping an eye on it."

Pinch, in the middle of the lane, stopped and turned to face her.

"Dolly Johnson, cover yourself properly, go indoors and go to bed," he advised.

"I said, I'm keeping an eye on Laurel Cottage. If they think they're going to creep in and out, without my noticing, they'll have to be more clever than most."

"There is nothing going on across the road, and if I hear any gossip I shall know where to come. Now, go to bed, Dolly Johnson."

She was cross. "Ooh, you're in a bad mood," she said nastily. She pulled the flimsy wrap across her bust and made a show of tying the string of her petticoat over her waist before turning her back. She marched, the flopping heels of her slippers keeping a ragged time. She slammed her front door, rattled the old fashioned window shutters closed and, though Pinch was already too far up The Street to be bothered, she brought the wind-up gramophone to the table and played it without the sock in it.

Only Gort's dog barked.

Others were quiet in their houses. Too early for most of them to be in bed, husbands, wives, and widows were reading by the light of standard lamps or, in Judith Cart's case, eating cheap chocolates on her own. Pinch knew that some, like Edna Carstairs and Mary in the Post Office, stayed awake with their books or needlework until three or four in the morning. Others - especially Poppy Anders, now poorly, and Eliza Knightly, now gone - liked to work on their back steps by the light of a good moon. Small Thin Annie, neither four feet eleven nor eight stones, was worrying over her account of the benefit evening for the Reading Room. The village knew that they had collected seven pounds; hurrying hands had counted it before going home. So where had the extra shilling and five pence come from? She must remember to thank Reverend Skillet from the neighbouring parish for supplying the piano at short notice. That was a simple enough task but it was no help in solving the one and five pence mystery. She wouldn't talk to anyone about it, so it worried her silly until Harvest Sunday.

Pinch proceeded. Only Queen O'Scots was watching intently enough to notice a slight kick in his port-side step as if he had a stone in his boot or had learned to keep his circulation up.

Tall and lanky Jacoby, with his hands well below his trouser pockets, was waiting against the churchyard wall with a crooked walking stick that made him look like someone from a nursery rhyme. He could keep still like no other man, so that any observer would look twice and decide no-one was there. Jacoby walked by night. "You've got a job for me, Arthur?" he said when his friend was safely within earshot.

"My God, you've a face like walnut," said the policeman. Jacoby was new, but Pinch had known him on a previous beat. Of course, both had been younger then and too often on different sides of the law.

"Old doctors said my visage had the hue and texture of brains." He tapped the ground with the foot of his stick and listened, with no more comment than a nod of his elongated chin.

Pinch said, "Advice, Jacoby. I want to know what you make of some footprints. It's clear to me that Spinster Knightly came out of doors last night in her carpet slippers. She walked up the Waddie and got as far as this junction. Then, I'm not sure."

Without further talk, the pair reviewed the evidence. In two or three places, Jacoby stooped to look closer. Only once, did he stand and stroke his whiskery chin in indecision. "Carpet slippers?" he queried.

"No doubt in my mind," Pinch said. "Safest way an old woman has of keeping quiet."

"Meeting someone?"

Pinch countered. "What do you think?"

"No sign of it. But when she got to this junction, she took off her slippers and went barefoot for five yards. Hardly enough to get her to the top of Back Lane."

"Ah, I'd not noticed that." Pinch got down on all fours, then flexed his elbows until he was prone on the ground. "Yes, it does seem the same size."

"If you get out of the way, I'll lift that print for you."

"Our obliging doctor should be able to match it against the corpse."

"Won't your Detective Officers be wanting it left untouched?" said the wise old keeper as he worked.

"Only if they ask." Pinch collected his thoughts. "So, if she wasn't here to meet someone, after hours, she came looking for something."

"That maybe, if she had her face down." Jacoby was on his feet again, wrapping the evidence in a blue and grey handkerchief. "But if she looked up, she'd be looking not 'for' but 'at'."

"Good Lord," they both said as they lifted their eyes.

They were looking at the lamp shining from Mavis Reynolds' back bedroom, where the lady was dancing in her veils. "Like no woman dances unless someone is watching," said Jacoby.

"But then, whoever was admiring the show was watching in the dark."

"But it can't be more than a guess."

"But it's possible," said Pinch, "and while it's possible, it's the only curious lead I've got."

The policeman lit his pipe. He held the fingers of both hands over the bowl so that it looked as if he was conjuring smoke from his palms, like magic.

"You could begin by asking about her source of faggies. Mavis Reynolds is closer to a full set than the rest of us put together. Lord knows where she's getting them from. No woman can smoke enough to pick up that many."

"I'll see what I can do," Pinch said with a smile. The two men had started their way back to the churchyard. "I don't collect them myself but I've picked up Monza, Southport and the Winter Grand Prix."

30

The gamekeeper needed no time to think. "No good to me, Arthur. You haven't got Number Twenty-One, have you?"

Pinch shook his head.

"Keep me in mind if you come across it."

Pinch was noted for insisting that he knew no man with a better mind than Jacoby for putting things together. "There's nothing for you here, Pinch," said the gamekeeper, unknowingly reflecting some earlier advice from Doctor Meriweather. "I thought we'd find some trace of a witch's old familiar. You've always got to wonder when an old woman dies on her own, like that."

"Don't come with that rubbish."

"Ah, country rot is it? Well, Arthur Pinch, there is something that you're no expert on. I'll tell you. You can't solve this killing, if a killing's what you have, and not be wary of the old lore." He clapped his friend on his back. "Go home and get yourself to my shed for half past five and the best of breakfasts will be waiting for you."

"Johnny Murderer is getting too clever these days," Pinch complained, in spite of himself. His way was to keep to himself any views he had on controversial matters. The village did not want to be bothered by his pontifications. "He predicts how the evidence," he continued, "will be presented in court, then plans the killing so that none of the jigsaw fits."

"This Liverpool business, you mean."

"Thank God, the courts saw through it. The man Wallace was never guilty. But the one who got away? Now, he was too clever for any country that relies on evidence. Goodnight, Jake."

Pinch was ready to walk alone down Back Lane, but he was distracted by the rattle and farting of an underpowered motorcycle, struggling along the unmade surface of Wretched Lane. Pinch thought about hurrying into the lane and holding an arm in the air, bringing the delinquent to an emergency stop, but he was too far away. When the motorbike reached the junction where three roads came together, the errant rider steered along the footpath at the top of the green and onto Vicarage Lane. He disappeared through the vicarage gates and Pinch said to himself, "Our new vicar. I shall have words. We can't be putting up with motorcycles riding around the village lanes after dark." He walked a few paces before adding the postscript, "Young fool."

He took his time, keeping a proper patrol pace, down Back Lane, (pronounced Bach Lane if you lived there,) through the pitch black Twitchels and into The Street. He paused at the stony pull-in, where tomorrow's bus for the market was parked, and there smoked another pipe. Before he was done, the last of the lights went out and his village closed her eyes in the lee of its murder.

Chapter Three

Tea in Town

Eight miles north of Peggy's village, in a place of hidden commerce, the four narrow floors of Templar Simms and Harcourt stood as part of an uneven terrace at the bottom of a perpetually mucky market place. Squashed between a greengrocery and a timber factor, Templars was disproportionate, uneven and readily overlooked. And, because it was three feet behind the building line, the home of the town's longest established solicitor looked as if it were skulking. People said that because Templar Simms and Harcourt had been here for more years than any other lawyers, their socks and turn-ups were deeper in the muddier waters of the town. Sometime ago, the names had been painted white on the inside of a first floor window, but the grime of the place had got to them so that most had turned flaky, all had turned grey and one or two had inexplicably slipped out of line. Something resembling Jacob Marley's knocker had been screwed to the front door, but few people used it; it was better to walk in rather than be caught waiting on Templars' doorstep. Only people with disreputable secrets would call at such a place. Old Harcourt spoke of the shame which burns a hole in the purses of good men and, although old Harcourt had been dead for two generations, the wizards, scribes and money-tellers in Templar's domain still washed their hands in the same sinks. This stretch of High Street, with its narrow uneven pavements and leaning lampposts, had claim on a nugget of historical trivia. This was the first road, beyond London, where Waiting Limitation was shared between the sides of the street and the days of the week. There was No Waiting outside Templars on Wednesday and Friday, while the opposite side of the street had a restriction on Monday and Tuesday. (Thursday was Early Closing.) But most passengers along the High Street were not concerned about parking, or street-lamps or cracked and sloping paving. Drains. Drains were in the newspaper columns, most letters to the council and on the tip of every tongue. Drains. The word hung in the air; it was a catch in the throat and a sniff beneath nostrils, young and old. 'The drains are good tonight.' 'Close the window, mam; you're letting in the drains.' 'Ah, that'll be them drains.'

George Templar, tall, linear and long limbed, worked with forty volumes of law on his desk; he flitted from one to another with all the fluster of a clergyman wanting to annotate his sermon. On the back of the office door, a brown raincoat clung to a hook, without a hanger, and lent an odour to the room, rather like the woody, smoky scent offered to a country house by an old long-haired hound who has laid for too long in front of a cupboard beneath the staircase. Templar's aptitude for disorder, bad manners and dribbling from his nose added to the chaos. A cup and saucer of tea stood on one pile of books, a file of letters for signature was held between two volumes of another and the photograph of his wife had dropped to the carpet. This had found the ideal spot of carpet for ash shaken from his cigarettes, so he placed the Brickwoods Ales ashtray on Mrs. Templar's face. 'Mr George' worked with his phone in the lap of his trousers.

When the office door opened and the light changed from dirty yellow to musty yellow, his eyelids came down, hooding his jaundiced eyes. He spoke over his clerk's announcement of the visitor and jabbed a long nailed, discoloured and sausage shaped finger, indicating where the applicant should stand. Usually, he opened each interview with a curt, "State your purpose," but, in this case, he wanted to know nothing of the woman's reason for calling on him. Jump! he reminded himself. George Templar is expected to jump and greet with an outstretched hand.

Instead: "I've been expecting you," he said without taking the cigarette from his mouth. A file of old papers was open in front of him, kept safe by a woolly tag in one corner. A willow patterned plate of ham and mustard sat on top of the papers. Templar was eating between puffs, with a fork and a spoon which he used like a toddler's pusher. "I've had to take advice. People are very interested." Sun came through the office window and glinted gold as it bounced on the crown of his balding head and went back out again. Sunshine had no business here.

Peggy, standing in front of him, both hands holding her handbag over her tummy, said, "I've come for the letters."

"Of course," he nodded, disrupting the light without spoiling the effect. Then he explained, as if she hadn't been keeping up, "That's what I've been expecting. The thing is …"

"Miss Knightly always said that I was to have the letters and I am sure you have them in your safe."

"Of course," he nodded again. Surely, this woman couldn't suspect that he was ignorant of these matters. "I sent my secretary to collect them on the evening of the old lady's passing."

"The Coroner still hasn't released the body."

"Please sit down. I cannot abide women who hover."

Peggy Pinch apologised, then told herself off for doing so. She looked around, reached backwards to tip the office cat from the only armchair and settled herself in its place.

Ash dropped from the tip of Templar's cigarette to the open page of the book propped against the front pile. Incredibly, he had been reading. "The content of the letters means that they remain of interest to our military. You see, during the war our Eliza Knightly corresponded with a German boyfriend. The mail was quickly intercepted and Eliza agreed to particular arrangements in order to escape prosecution. She submitted all future letters to the War Office, who translated them into German, adding extra titbits which they wanted her German soldier to read. His replies were treated similarly. The War Office noted their content and Eliza received English translations only a few days later. It worked well for nearly two years."

The cat had jumped into Peggy's lap and she was soothing the fur in the pit of its front leg. "Miss Knightly was convinced that her lover was betrayed by someone who still lives in our village," she said. "I'm afraid the hatred consumed her. I spent hours talking it over with her and she never changed her mind. I promised that I would take possession of the letters, examine them in detail and, hopefully, identify the spy in our midst. I have to say that I don't hold out much hope but it was my promise and I shall do it carefully."

"The thing is," he began but paused deliberately. He opened a drawer, at his left knee, and took a pinch of cheese from a concealed saucer. "The War Office want you to report any suspicions through me. I am, so to speak, the go-between. That is to say, me and not the police. Your diligence is not unknown to our military mandarins and they see an advantage in the investigation being led by someone in the village. But unmasking a spy is not a simple matter. There is always the broader context. It may suit our War Office to leave the naughty miscreant in place, for example. Simple folk, like you and me, cannot expect to grasp the subtleties. Lordie-be, we're not meant to." A man with any humour might have laughed at this point.

Peggy stared at him. "The Coroner hasn't released the body," she repeated.

"The Coroner has an interest in the letters. Of course, he has."

"Do you own a blue racing car? And why didn't you keep your appointment at Wayback Cottage? You were supposed to be taking an inventory."

He removed his spectacles. His eyelids had a red trim where they met his eyeballs; they turned faintly yellow as they watered. "I'm thinking, who is this proud woman - no, a presumptuous woman who comes to my office expecting confidence and consideration? True - it is true that I've heard she is the woman of a village policeman. A village policeman of some standing, due - I am told - to his tally of arrests for rural murder. Does she - I mean to say, can she delight in reflected glory of this service? I believe she does but, ah, the truth of it. Yes, the truth is what we must divine. Yes, I can hear the constable - in his cardigan, I should think, or his pyjama jacket, I mean pulled decently over some regular clothing. Yes, the doors to their cottage are locked and gas lamps are turned low, when he asks for any village slurry that might be passing through. Is that it? She deals in vestry gossip, does she? And here she is. I've come for the letters, she demands, and why hasn't the Coroner released the Knightly corpse? And Templar, whose portfolio of service to the nation is not entirely empty, must --- jump!"

He shouted, "Templar must jump!" and shot to his feet so that the telephone fell from his lap to the carpet. He reached down, pulled it by the twisted cord to its receiver and dialled a single digit.

"Just a second of your time, Miss Twinn."

He sat and resumed his smoke. "The Coroner and the Chief Constable are fully cognisant of the arrangement. I am sure your husband will want to check. Mrs. Pinch, I did not put myself forward as your contact in the matter of your investigation. I want you to know that."

The cat purred. An urban pigeon, discoloured and too fat, landed on the ledge of the closed window and brought the familiar croak up from his throat - 'my big toe does hurt' - while looking around for somewhere else to flit to. George Templar, acting as if his main job was to consolidate the impression of a horrible man, picked up a glass paperweight and rapped it on the window pane. The pigeon with the big toe flew off.

Deborah Twinn was used to walking in without a knock. Peggy Pinch thought 'My Goodness' as she looked up from the low cushion of her chair. Miss Twinn was what American detectives would call 'well-stacked.' She had been taught to deport herself powerfully. Her shoulders she held back, pushing her bust forward. Her elbows were kept in and it was always 'nose before toes'. She walked in a way that emphasised her balance. And, she had been told, balance was elegance. She was a fortunate woman who could wear dresses two sizes too small or, at least, too tight. Peggy thought, 'No stays or corsets or laces up the back for this Miss Prim-Twinn - just the tough love of a liberty bodice with, maybe, a touch of elasticated rubber.'

Templar was saying, "Miss Twinn, you cancelled my visit to Wayback Cottage on the afternoon of Eliza Knightly's death."

"On Miss Knightly's instruction. She telephoned at lunch time."

This was a rough and ready town. It wasn't a community that attracted the professions or those who thought they were on the way up. Peggy was sure that every townswoman wanted to wipe the smile from Miss Twinn's haughty face but the policeman's wife pictured a different notion. She wanted to stand behind Miss Twinn in a queue and pinch her bottom. And when the woman turned around, she would catch only Peggy's mask of preoccupation. She was sure she could pinch half a dozen times and not be suspected.

"And you're sure it was Miss Knightly? It could have been the murderer wanting to keep me out of the way."

"Has Miss Knightly been murdered, Mr Templar? She definitely telephoned, sir; I had quite a conversation with her. She was thinking of submitting dahlias to a village competition. Have you finished with lunch, Mr Templar?"

"Not quite." He drove the spoon around his plate, pressing some ham and mustard against the fork. Peggy could not look at him without picturing purple grapes on the turn. He was explaining, "Miss Twinn is partial to a dahlia in a pot," as the young woman walked out of the office.

George Templar cleared his throat. "Yes, I am the blue racing car. I was curious about the cancellation and, having no alternative appointments, I decided to take a drive to your village. When I saw the commotion, I - well, I decided to drive on." He was still looking at the door which had closed on Miss Twinn. "A little more thought and I would have gone uphill. The car is not built for downhill runs. You will note that she has twice completed the Shelsey hill-climb in fifty-two seconds"

"The Coroner hasn't released the body."

"Indeed, and here we intrude into police business but I suppose there's no harm in mentioning it. Rather as an after thought, the doctor decided to take a sample of blood. Miss Pinch, your spinster friend was poisoned. You have a murderer in the village."

Peggy shook her head. "But there's no investigation going on. Where are the detectives, the superior officers and paper clerks?"

"Quite." He bowed his head until his nose was all but brushing the page edges of Shannon on Trespass. "Oh, quite, quite. You are quite right." He cleared his throat again. "Because of the circumstances - that is to say, the military interest in what you might uncover in the letters - the Coroner has delayed the inquest. You have until next Tuesday. After that, the constabulary takes over and the letters receive the protection of Crown evidence."

He had intended this announcement to conclude the interview but Peggy wasn't ready to leave. She looked around and tried to take in the curious sense of the room. The textured wallpaper had been spoiled with a pale wash (which lifted the paper from the walls in places) and the carpet, so obviously brought in from somewhere else, was threadbare in all the wrong places. There was nothing authentic about George Templar's work place; it was - and she searched for the phrase - 'put together'.

She said, almost without thinking, "Murder, mustard and cheese."

Templar creased his forehead as he looked up from his papers. "What's that?"

"This office is all about murder, mustard and cheese."

"Go lightly with the murder," he said, making little of her remark. "We've not had a body in this office since '74. Two brothers accused each other of stealing some church plate. One shot the other and the booty was never found." He added, "The old bugger died just where you are sitting, though not in the same chair. They had to buy a new one."

Peggy shifted uneasily but smiled.

"As for the rest, Miss Twinn is as keen as mustard and, like cheese, I give most people indigestion." He looked up, "So please, let me know if I can do you a disservice."

Peggy was shown to the High Street through a side door; she was sure that any passers-by might think that she had been up to something grubby. Tea at the Templars had been cheap and bitter and she was so determined to find a lovely cuppa that, at first, she hurried past the cake shop. On second thoughts, she waited patiently in the queue and bought four cheese scones from the display (which was an extravagance because she knew she would manage no more than two). Her favourite tea shop was only a few yards further on where she found a corner table to herself.

Two young women, dressed in their frilly aprons and black uniforms to make them look like Corner House Nippies, knew that Mrs. Pinch liked to settle down before ordering. This half hour rush before the mid-morning lull was so busy that being allowed to leave a customer alone for several minutes was something of a relief.

"I wonder. Might I share your table?"

The woman was a few years younger. She wore a yellow and grey summer dress (more flared than the fashion) a faux straw hat with berries stitched to the band, and white gloves.

Unnecessary gloves, thought Peggy.

She was fair, with curly auburn hair and the tawny cheeks of a face that had only recently out grown their freckles.

"Of course, you may. That would be very nice."

"I was here when you put a dead mouse down the back of that lady's dress. It was so wonderful. Seriously, I don't think anyone else saw you. But I did. Oh, what a riot! Of course, you had made good your getaway; you wouldn't have seen the fuss." Peggy thought the young woman was going to clap her hands in delight. "Oh, what a to-do. I believe I've loved you ever since."

"My, my. My own appreciation society. Shall I have membership cards printed and distribute a quarterly newsletter?"

The woman smiled. "The P.P.A.S. How wonderful."

A waitress was at her shoulder. "Any special order, madam, or just your usual choice?"

"Yes, there is something special." Peggy produced the paper bag of scones. "I'd like you to warm these and bring the smallest pot of mustard."

"Mustard, ma'am. We do use the best variety of butters."

Peggy showed a puzzled face.

"The mustard, madam? People usually spread the faintest trace to disguise the taste of cheap margarines. I wanted to assure you that we only use butter."

"Oh, I am sure you do, but please bring the mustard. The smallest of portions."

The waitress withdrew and the woman leaned forward. "My name is Lettice. Mother always said that I should find a man called Sandwich. Then I could be Lettice Sandwich. But I didn't. I married George Templar."

"Oh, I've just been --- but you know that, don't you?"

"That's what it's all about, really. I am afraid to say, there's carryings-on going on."

"Carryings-on?"

Lettice nodded. "They've been going on for months."

Tea and scones with mustard arrived. "I've brought a pot for two in case your friend would like a cup. The manageress says there's a charge for only one, of course."

"Thank you, my dear."

The women sat quietly while the waitress arranged the spread. Lettice leaned forward to say, "I am sorry about the drains."

"They're not your fault, are they?"

"No, but I live here and you don't, so it's my place to apologise."

"Your husband is having an affair with Miss Twinn?" asked Peggy.

Lettice nodded. "Prim-Miss-Twinn. I'd like you to put a dead mouse down her back."

"I've done that only once," Peggy chuckled. "And, I promise you, I didn't get away with it. Well, not completely."

"They go to the pictures every Tuesday teatime. Then they come back to the office for an hour in the dark. I will let you in before they arrive. You can hide and, when they start to cuddle, you can creep up behind them and drop the dead mouse down her back."

"That would be very difficult to get right," said Peggy.

"I want her to know, that's all. I don't mind her carrying on with my husband. Good lord, I don't love the man; I never have. But I want her to know that I know all about it."

Quietly, Peggy Pinch was working something out in her head. 'I will need a good escape plan,' she thought.

"I know what you're thinking," said Lettice Templar. "How could this girl have married an oaf like him?"

Peggy was nodding. "His money, I was thinking. You did get your hands on his money, I suppose."

Now they were experimenting with synchronised nodding. "I was quite famous for spending his money, but there were other attractions."

Peggy recollected the yellow fingernails. "I can't imagine any."

"Oh, Mrs. P, have you never watched a horror picture and wondered what it would be like if the monster asked you to dance? Have you never heard a noise in the night and kept absolutely still so that the ghost might slip into your bed? Like the ghost of old Harcourt, horrid beyond horrible. There is a nature of love that relies on a feeling of fear."

"How long does it last?" Peggy asked doubtfully.

"You've heard people say that it's not until your married that you find out that he cannot put his socks away or that he has to place his teaspoon on the mantelpiece instead of its saucer. You know the sort of things that make romance difficult. But I am not wanting that kind of romance. In every horror picture, the most vulnerable girl refuses to betray the monster. That's the kind of commitment that I'm talking about." Lettice Templar did not recognise the contradiction that wormed its way, like a roughly tied knot, into the root of Peggy's mind. In Lettice's story, it was not the monster who was being betrayed."

"I just want to -- Mrs. Pinch, I want to fight back."

Peggy was thinking, 'If I could persuade someone from the village, a motorcar driver, to wait by the kerb for twenty minutes. Wait, with the engine running. They could whisk me away. It would be after dark, of course.'

She glanced at the wall clock above the service door. She needed to get back to the village. She had hoped to make friends with the dressmaker who worked in the back room of the milliner's shop, but that would have to wait for another day.

Desk Sergeant Bernard Hawk rarely went out on patrol these days. He argued that a good policeman has no need to seek information; it comes to him, as if secrets were drawn to the familiar blue lamp at every police porch. But, that morning, he was taking a slow walk from the station to the market square where he stood still, establishing an unnerving presence. Hawk had forsaken the comfort of his enquiry office because Constable Pinch had telephoned late last night and they had both agreed that Peggy Pinch required supervision. Policemen's wives, said Hawk, who had never married, are like puppy dogs; they may be trusted until they think for themselves.

He was tall, sturdy and tough and was feared by errant schoolboys, incompetent burglars and inebriated veterans alike. His head, thick like a bull's, was so large that although his helmet was the largest in the quartermaster's store, it looked some sizes too small.

The driver of the unmarked Morris five hundredweight van drew up at the far kerb and acknowledged him with a squawk of his motor horn. Sergeant Hawk stayed still, except for an index finger which he raised with the solemnity of a cricket umpire awarding a wicket. The vehicle was designated for general fetch and carry purposes. This morning, it would ferry the weekly box of documents and a policeman's wife to Arthur Pinch's sleepy parish.

Hawk didn't know why Pinch had not gone further in his career. True, he had come to his village under a cloud but such scars are soon forgotten; certainly, they last no longer than the tenure of one chief. Although his wife was known to have a mind for murder, Pinch still had a good copper's brain. He could sense when things were wrong and his thorough grounding in the basics meant that he could easily put himself in the right place to sniff out the truth. Hawk liked the man's pastoral approach; he often called his beat his parish, and his job was more about looking after the village than purging it of its transgressions.

The sergeant sniffed in the cold.

Just recently, Hawk had been busy reminding his superiors of these qualities of Arthur Pinch, because Arthur Pinch's 'sleeping dog' had stirred and wanted to stretch his limbs as forward and wide as they could reach. The sleeping dog was the matter of Pinch's retirement which would entail, unless diverted, turfing the couple out of the police house. There had been some expectation that Peggy's mother had made provision in her will but the old lady had died before her daughter's marriage and Hawk's enquiries confirmed that she had died intestate and penniless. "Well, now, Hawk. It's up to you," the Under-

Superintendent had declared. "Come on, old man. Address the problem with some imagination."

Sergeant Hawk was not without imagination, although he held the distinction of having failed more auditions for the constabulary Christmas pantomime than any other officer. He did not see how a fanciful approach could apply to the recruitment, retention and disposals regulations of a police force. The manual was all about money, a particularly arid landscape for anyone in search of jokes. Then he recalled the advice of an old and wise Special, of military background, that no regulation should be acted upon until a contrary regulation could be found. While their juxtaposition rarely allowed more than a moment of humour, it sometimes gave way to common sense.

Chapter Four
Six English Villagers

Maud Nevers, tarnished and wrinkly, weary and naked in Doctor Meriweather's bed, kicked the last of the fuzzy flannelette sheets off the mattress and leaned a little to one side so that her freckled breasts came together in a filled out shape. She crossed her forearms to conceal her protruding nipples, each had the look and the colour of Doctor Hazel's Menthol Lozenges. She wasted a little time thinking. Then she lay on her tummy and pressed her knees down, lifting her pelvis from the mattress. She went up on her elbows and, again, her breasts fell free. She showed them off.

But all this had no effect. Meriweather wasn't there to make the best of them. Always, he made the excuse of needing the bathroom, then went for a smoke in his dining room and he didn't come back. This had been episode three of their affair and she had allowed it only because she believed the old wives' tale that a revisit would flush away any seed that might already be growing.

God, he disgusted her. She loathed the little red hairs on the back of his neck which grew to long whiskers on his back, like appendages on daddy long legs. His odour turned her stomach. It was the smell of a closed up furniture shop and it got mustier as he got close to finishing the job. She hated the pitted skin on the bulb of his nose. And, always, he was best interested in her bottom in the middle of lovemaking. Most of all, she hated the cruelty of his wanting nothing to do with her afterwards.

Lying nude upstairs would get her no cups of tea; she might as well get up and make one for herself. She kicked her legs high in the air and in one jump her feet were on the painted floorboards.

She supposed that people knew. She hoped that they had made the wrong guess and knew less than they thought. It had been weeks now but still, she hadn't decided what to do. Hours of trying to come up with a plan got no further than hoping that her nicest thoughts would come true. "That's Mau' Nevers for you," she said as she wept at the top of Doctor Meriweather's staircase. Her venture downstairs to make tea had progressed no further. "Too busy with daydreams to face reality." She felt unable to share her troubles with anyone in the village. That was the worst of it. Doctor Meriweather? She was determined that he must be the last person to find out. He was sure to know his own ways of solving the problem, and Maud could never do that. "Such a pickle," she sighed. She remembered that she had a niece in Rotherham but nieces in Rotherham seemed too obscure an option. Of course, most people in the village would expect her to marry Willie Wheeler. And Willie might expect that too. But Maud had never thought of catching a husband by baking an early bun in the oven. This wasn't at all what she wanted.

Peggy Pinch was back in the village as Queen O'Scots was crossing from the schoolma'ams gate to the Post Office. The cat did not acknowledge her but paused, cocked an ear, then sat in the middle of the lane. It was two in the afternoon. This was a lane where murder had been done yet folk seemed determined to make little of it. It was a business better kept indoors.

Pinch was standing by the churchyard wall where The Street, Wretched Lane and Back Lane came together. He always looked like the best sort of policeman when he had nothing to do, thought Peggy. Mary, the postmistress, had turned the closed sign on her shop door and Miss Reynolds, for whom the Post Office queue was the engine of life, wondered if she should lean against the window ledge and wait for someone to come along. But leaning looked so slovenly and said too much about one's character.

Peggy thought that the day went sluggishly, as if the village had suffered a rain storm; now that it was over, neighbours were prepared to come out of doors and do what needed to be done, but their heads stayed down and looked for no conversation. Then the District Nurse arrived, seated correctly upright on her bicycle, her hat pinned to the top of her head and her black shoes fit for any parade ground. She parked against the Post Office wall and announced herself with a crisp 'Good morning,' ignoring the Closed sign as she strode into the shop.

Securing Nurse Everard's services had not been complicated but sufficiently convoluted to test Meriweather's patience. Poppy Anders was on his regular list yet her funds would not run to the day-to-day attendance of a nurse. But neither was she a panel patient. Indeed Poppy was a property owner and drew little sympathy from several panel members who rented their homes. "Time, gentlemen, is not on our side," the doctor had pointed out and, with good grace, the panel sanctioned the assignment of Miss Everard.

Peggy meant to introduce herself but a shrill cry from Dolly Johnson got in the way of that. "Coo-ee!" the woman beckoned. "This way, Peggy Pinch." She was trotting up from the step of her side door. Today, the busy-body wore a home-made housekeeper's smock of thin grey and green stripes, and she had spent the morning setting her hair in silly ringlets. As Peggy walked towards the gate of Little Firs, she noticed Jamie Eider - yes, she needed to talk to him - resting on the bank by the ford, at the bottom of The Street; he had been on a three hour cycle ride.

"You know that he has an eye for you." Dolly was talking too loud but Peggy didn't shush her. "You do know that, don't you?"

"Little Jamie? How sweet." Then, "Dear Dolly, who are you talking about?"

"Where were you going? I must say, you've got a gormless look on your face."

"The vicarage."

They both knew that Peggy had been walking down The Street, away from the church and its vicarage.

"You won't find any vicars there. Not these days. Our vicar spends too much time in another person's house. That's the truth. Come on, I'll step along with you up the Waddie." They walked to the end of Dolly's back garden, through the iron gate and onto the rough, unmade foot path that went muddy after every shower of rain. "Reynolds will follow, but we should be able to talk if we keep in front. Your Mr Pinch says I'm to make nothing of it. He says that nothing's going on in Laurel Cottage with our new vicar. But what does he know?" Dolly paused, looked back along the rough and ready path. "She's hiding," she said.

"Dolly, what do you *know*?"

"Sir Roland's got the itch for you," was the emphatic reply. "He minces no words. He says it, straight out ..."

"Then he ought to mind his tongue."

They were making good progress up the unmade Waddie, with its furrows and ditches and holes dug out years before.

"If you're going to the vicarage, you'll have to deal with Polly. Have you met her yet? She's not like dealing with the new vicar himself."

Peggy paused to look at the musty, red brick building with its strange attics and turrets; it was a house of at least three secret passages and one dangerously forgotten staircase.

"Vicarage maids. They are often like that. It's because they sleep in weird places," Peggy suggested.

Polly Adam - she would correct you if you added an 's' - had lain heavily on one side during the moments of her delivery so that, through life, she had to hold a lazy shoulder slightly forward. She liked to lay the forearm across her belly. Folk said that Polly Adam looked up at you from a bottom corner. She had black hair, flecked with premature grey, brushed straight back and bound in a tail that fell half way down her back. Well rounded cheeks, a squashed mouth and pointed nose gave her something of a mouse-like face.

"You didn't ought to come round the back, Mrs. Pinch," she said, as nicely as she could. "Sullivan would tell you himself, if he were here which he isn't and not likely to be before four o'clock, tea time. He'd say that the likes of you should call at the front door and I should welcome you in." Polly had interrupted her preparation of green-groceries for the vicar's dinner. She had cut her thumb; some blood ran down the outside of the stone sink, some blood trickled into the water.

Peggy noticed that Tuesday morning was in capitals on the wall calendar; she wondered what needed doing to merit such emphasis. "Tuesday morning," she remarked more loudly than she meant to.

"Yes, yes. I mustn't forget. Tuesday morning."

She led Peggy through the scullery and into the large hallway where the main staircase rose in three tiers, like the main edifice of the parish.

"You've hurt your face," Peggy enquired.

"It looks much worse than it is. Farmer Wistow gave me a sparrow hawk. He'd heard how much I love to sport with them. I'm afraid she caught me as she was settling on me when we weren't used to each other. Accidents in the early days are common enough. Tell me, does it look like the Mark of Cain?"

Peggy winced. It looked livid. "Yes, it does," she said. "I think you ought to get it looked at."

"Doctor Meriweather called last evening. He says he'll keep an eye on it. Why are you here, Mrs. Pinch?" Adding, "I rather like the Mark of Cain. It sounds like witchcraft and all that to do. Tell me, how did you know about Tuesday?"

"I read it on your calendar. I'm sorry. I can't help being nosy."

"It's something of mine that I want to do by myself."

"Of course, Polly, I have to do some studying which is very private business."

"Mr Sullivan would be pleased to hear it, Mrs. Pinch. The Bible, is it?"

"No, I suppose you could call it family business but I need to be quiet and away from prying eyes."

"Then I'll show you the Dead Bishop's Sitter. Come through the ladies' parlour and we'll use the second stairs." She said, as Peggy followed, "You'll be able to see your husband through the round window as we go up. He's standing beneath the churchyard yew."

"Oh yes. Yes, I see." She still found it hard to look at Arthur Pinch on duty without feeling proud.

"Mrs. Pinch, I'm pleased you've come. I wonder, can I ask you to spend a few minutes with Little Annie Preacher? Twice, she's called on Sullivan when he's been out and I'd rather not bother him with such a trivial worry. She's puddling her head over the Lipton's Tea coupons that she used to give to Spinster Knightly."

"Of course, I'll put her mind at rest, and you're quite right, our vicar's busy enough without tea wrappers."

From the first creak of its opening, Peggy loved the Dead Bishop's Sittingroom. It was small, and lined with books except for the far wall which was a window, from tip to toe, divided into twelve panes. The bottom row was large. The next was middle sized and the top two rows were small.

"The table's far too broad for the space," said Polly, "but I suppose they needed to place it."

"No, no. I shall need a large table top. Polly, what an adorable little room. Will the vicar mind if I work in here on Wednesday morning? It's private, you see."

"Oh, Mr Sullivan won't mind at all. He's such a nice man; I've never known him say no. I've not had one that's so grateful for what little I do for him. I shall make sure a jug of lemon squash is on the table and I'll bring a pot of tea now and then."

Twenty minutes later, Peggy and Pinch were sitting alone in the church nave. It was a long time since they had done this. They chose a far pew, half way up the aisle, where a pillar of crumbly stone obscured their view of the pulpit. Pinch thought, I must remember this for Sundays. Peggy was anxious that someone might be in the vestry but, no, Pinch assured her that they were quite alone. She looked up at the high roof and across to the noteworthy window, close to the Sunday school door. "This place always seems -" she waited for the right word to come to her - "Empty. It has an empty taste to it, and the smell."

"Good lord, don't tell the new vicar that. He's struggling as it is." He tried to put a kindly edge to his voice: "Poppy Anders has accepted that she has only a few days with us. That's why she has shut herself away; she'll see only Doctor Meriweather and the Reverend."

"The telephone call was to her nephew?"

Pinch nodded. "She made her farewells with Eliza Knightly last week. Heaven alone knows how long they had been friends."

"She's heard of the murder?"

"Both Meriweather and Sullivan have managed to keep that from her. The young vicar has made an extraordinary effort. She doesn't know a waking hour when he's not at her bedside."

"Pinch, I'd love to know what she's been saying to him."

"My Peggy, that would change the whole nature of our village." He was sitting with his helmet on his knees and his truncheon, which always lay heavily in its pocket, on the wooden seat beside him. Three times, he caught his hand venturing into

55

his tunic's right-hand pocket. He longed for a smoke. Perhaps, because he was in church but not at a service, he was allowed -- no, this wasn't the place to light up his pipe.

She was saying, "I know. I wouldn't want Sullivan to break their confidence. But I need your help, Pinch. I need your mind, your memories and your stories of the old village. London has passed to me Miss Knightly's letters and I am supposed to work out who betrayed her lover."

Pinch nodded. A telephone call from Sergeant Hawk had brought him up to date.

"So, who's still here who lived through the war?"

"You and me." Again, he was fumbling with the pipe in his pocket.

"We don't count," Peggy was insisting.

Surely, an empty pipe offended no protocols. "Yes, we do. Or, at least, I do. You were too young but, at the time, many families suspected me of giving her up. Then, Edna Carstairs, Farmer Wistow, Dolly of course and the gamekeeper's grandfather."

"He's dead."

"Strictly, yes, but people like that carry their guilt from generation to generation."

"I'm not counting you or him," Peggy insisted.

"Are you counting Templar?"

"For certain."

"And little Sir Roland was at Winchester but home for the holidays. Include me - and you must - and you have Six English Villagers. Six English Villagers nosing in a hive, one went and stung himself."

"Sir Roland was just a child; he wasn't home long enough to know what was going on."

"And then there were five. Five English Villagers going in for law."

"I don't like that," said Peggy. "Try, made out of straw."

"One set himself on fire."

"Dolly. She's too much of a daydream to be a spy."

A black bird made the dash from one ceiling cove to another. The latch to the great door clunked. The husband and wife kept their heads down, not wanting conversation, as the footsteps kept to the far side of the font. They heard visitor take the age old key from the stone pillar and unlock the staircase to the tower.

"The verger?" Pinch wondered.

"I was counting on you to peep."

"But I was counting on you," he parried. "How far have we got?"

"And then there were four. Who's left?"

She could tell that Pinch was taking the game seriously. As he counted each name, he weighed their credibility as the culprit. "Edna Carstairs, Farmer Wistow, George Templar and Arthur Pinch."

"Grief, Pinch," she said, looking straight ahead. "Take your name out of the pie and it could be any one of them."

He said, allowing a moment between each word, "I don't quite see Edna Carstairs as Mata Hari."

"Which leaves Farmer Wistow and Templar the lawyer."

Pinch said at once, "Templar, every time."

"But, he can't be. Pinch, London has put him in charge of the case."

"That makes it twice as likely, I'd say." Pinch was ready to go. He shuffled his feet. He put his uniform straight. Then he sighed irritably, "My God, Peg. Can you feel them queuing up to tell us those 'somethings' that they're sure we need to know. People. You can't get away from them in this place. Eight hundred people stuck on an English hillside with a church at the top, and they can't pass their days without acquiring secrets. Secrets, that Arthur Pinch has got to be told."

Peggy was smiling. "Dr Meriweather has more to say. And what about Wistow? He's up and down The Street twice as often as he needs to be."

"I can feel them standing in line, just there behind my shoulder. Sir Roland of the Hall. I wonder what he's got to get off his chest. You know, there's nothing like murder for drawing dirty linen from the family chests." He stood still and sniffed the Autumn air. "You know, it's Sir Roland who gets my sympathy. He had a rotten home life, a rotten childhood, not to mention a rotten family. All round, he had a miserable start. So much expectation on his shoulders, so little help and he was quite alone. Do you remember his father? Do you remember seeing him?"

Peggy shook her head. "I can't have been more than ten years old. Byrivers Hall wasn't part of my playground."

"He was a hard man, hard to know, hard to get along with, hard to come up against." He took his pipe and tobacco pouch from his jacket pocket and set about charging it. Come four o'clock he wanted to be standing on the church green, a reliable figure puffing away as the village went about its business. "I don't think the lad had any chance of getting to know him."

"They can't have expected him to, if they sent him away to school," Peggy agreed.

"I don't know Sir Roland any better than others do, but I have always thought that he didn't grow up naturally."

Peggy agreed without thinking, "An odd ball."

"An odd ball indeed."

"We should expect anything from him." The policeman and his wife parted at the foot of the tower as the church clock struck four. "I'll be late tonight," he said, his toe bringing his bicycle pedal to its best position. "I've matters that need attention."

"Yes and I've been meaning to mention ... "

"Mention? Mention what you are up to? Oh, please, don't tell me what I don't need to know." He pushed on the pedal and was wheeling away, down the church path and only just managing the wooden gate.

Peggy found a familiar stone seat beneath leaves on the little patch of green and wasted five minutes gazing down The Street. Pinch was right, but Pinch was grumpy about it; she had always thought that the little settlement, out of anybody's way, was very English. Then, at times, - times like these, she supposed - the people in their little houses seemed to want nothing to do with the rest of the King's realm.

At that moment, the vicar was sitting down to an afternoon tea in his conservatory; cold chicken, salad, brie and farmhouse mustard. Edna Carstairs, in the old schoolma'am's cottage, was dusting flour on her kitchen table in preparation for pastry making. And Nevers, seated on the doctor's bottom stair, wrote a note for Mavis Reynolds.

As Peggy dawdled down the middle of the lane, she heard Jacoby's dog cart come up from behind. He passed with a growl, then deliberately picked up speed for the ford, on his way to his hatchery.

"You didn't see it," called Dolly Johnson, running up from her cottage gate. "That man rushing past you; he didn't make you think, did he?"

"Dolly, what?"

"You didn't think of this morning's front page."

"I've not had time."

"No, that's what I say. You didn't see the paper this morning."

"Dolly, let's get you settled indoors, shall we?"

"What were you looking for in Eliza Knightly's dead garden?"

"I wasn't looking for anything."

"Yes, you were," Dolly argued. "You were leaning over her little wall, then you looked up and really stretched your neck to look down her side path."

"I was looking for dahlias."

Dolly stepped back and frowned. "Dahlias? You won't find any dahlias in Miss Knightly's bed. You know what women thought about them in the war. Well, the war was everything to Miss Knightly so, definitely, she gardened without dahlias. Now are you going to listen to Dolly sensibly?"

"Dolly Sensibly," Peggy whispered. Life would be a whole lot easier if this was her name.

"There's a picture in the paper of that poor policeman, knocked over by a sporting car and killed. In Oxford, where the students are. And I was thinking, oh, our Mr Pinch was in Wayback Cottage, not two dozen yards from that blue racing car which came hurtling down our Street. It could have been our Pinch what was knocked down. Things had only to be a little bit different."

"Yes, wonderful." She had slipped her arm beneath Dolly's elbow so that she could guide her to her front garden. "Yes, well," she said softly. "I think the driver of that racing car might be getting his come-uppance before long."

"I hope so," Dolly insisted. "You see to it, Peggy."

She stopped and looked Peggy in the face.

"That's what your about, isn't it? You've got that man in mind for something. Oh, Peggy Pinch, you always have been a bugger!" Dolly Johnson laughed and skipped her way to the her garden shed. Where, she had tea.

Ginger-topped Jamie Eider, only eleven years old but so often Peggy's best little helper, was sitting on the back door step of the police house. He wore short trousers and an old school shirt which was eighteen months too small for him. One sock was turned over at the knee while the other had been pushed to his ankle so that he could scratch. His elbows were grazed and both knees bore the flaky scabs of old knocks and bumps. His toe caps were bulled like glass, because Jamie had devised his own shoe polish which he kept a-simmer in his own play shed. His dispensary, he called it.

He got to his feet as Peggy unlatched the back garden gate, and he gave the Boy Scout's salute. (There wasn't a Scout Troop within eight miles but Jamie adhered to the code.) "The maid in the vicarage. She said you wanted to see me."

"Did she? Did I? I mean, did I mention it?"

"You have a commission for me, Mrs. Pinch?"

"Come into my kitchen," she said. Without taking off her coat, she got the stove going and went to the cold larder where she poured a carton of lemon squash from the stone jar. "I've a cold pancake. Would you like to go halves, if I warm it through?"

He was scrambling onto a chair,. "Scrumptious," he said but held back from asking for sugar.

"I've some vicarage honey," Peggy added.

"I don't suppose we'll get any of that with the new vicar and all."

"Then we shall have to ask. You know, I think things are going to work out very well with our new Reverend."

"Tommy's feeling much better," he said. "He's too little to be my friend but I took him to play in the Twitchels yesterday afternoon. He didn't mention the thingy, so I let it be. We tried to swap some faggies but we had got similar numbers."

"Jamie, you didn't cheat him?"

"I shouldn't think so. He's as sharp as any of the lads. Besides, he's got a good collection. It's better than mine and he needs only a couple for a full house."

"I'm pleased you're looking after him, Jamie."

She busied herself with preparing the treat and, when she was seated at the table, he asked, "Are his mum and dad breaking up?"

"I don't know, dear."

"That's what people are saying and it's rotten if he doesn't know and everyone else does."

"I've a job for you, but word of it must go no further."

He fidgeted. "Of course, of course."

"I need some itching powder for grown-ups. It must be frightingly strong and, I'm sorry about this, but I need it straight away."

He was nodding already. "You need the dark red berries from the back of Miss Gort's hedge. I have a preparation already in my dispensary. Tell me, do you want it to bleed when it's scratched. Because, I can add some nibbles of thorns." He added gravely, "Mrs. Pinch, be wary, this is the strongest I have ever formulated."

"I am sure it will be perfect."

"And another thing, the lady that you want to itch, she will swell up, but only for a day or so,"

"Yes. Yes, that's very well thought out, Jamie. Now then, I am sure I've some pocket money, somewhere …"

"Money mustn't be involved," he protested at once. "You and I have worked together many times. I consider it a privilege to be of service."

By the time young Jamie scurried off, the cloudy Autumn evening had given way to a ghostly blue dusk which dampened the everyday sounds. When neighbours up The Street called their pets, or young children cried 'night night', it came down to Peggy in mumbles and murmurs from beneath the blankets. Still, there had been no arrests and the village was settling down to its second evening with a murderer in their midst.

Peggy watched Jamie cross The Street. She saw Edna Carstairs peering from the curtains of the Old Schoolma'am's Cottage; folk were looking out for one another. Peggy's footsteps sounded more distinct than they should have done as she walked to the side door of the police house. Then she was brought up by a grey shape bent over Pinch's contraption for producing compost. It was at the bottom of the garden, perhaps twenty yards away, but a trick of the light gave it a large shadow which swept the garden like the beam of a lighthouse scouring the night sky. At that moment, Dolly Johnson, three doors up, found something to laugh about and her goosie cackle rattled through the air. Peggy put out a hand to steady herself against the wall. She shuddered as the cat, fur on end, brushed against her calf. Queen O'Scots, like a witch's familiar, stepped forward to ward off wicked spirits, not two weeks before Hallowe'en.

"Please, who are you?" she said, taking an extra step, wanting common politeness to get the better of her girlish anxiety.

The shape formed into the figure of a man, straightening his back. He wore a grey tunic with a leather belt around its waist. "You're all right, Peggy Pinch. I'll not touch you. It's Sir Roland from Byriver Hall. I must show you something." For a Knight of the Realm, he looked suspiciously like a chauffeur. He had white unfeeling eyes that neither blinked nor looked anywhere but straight ahead. Devil's eyes, Peggy tried to stop thinking. She could prick them with cocktails sticks and they would give way, like the flesh of pulpy gooseberries. Those eyes would absorb the stabbing with no discomfort or obstruction.

"No, you can't come in. Constable Pinch isn't at home." Hastily, she added, "He will not be long."

"No, I don't want to. I want you to come to my house. I have information for you and something to show you. Something to give you, even."

Peggy was thinking fast. She didn't want to be indoors with him. "Then first, you must run me to town."

She thought, silly, that's worse.

"I've an errand to run. To Templars. You can wait outside." She could hear herself yapping like a ruffled terrier. "It won't take me long. And you must bring me back again."

"Of course. There's some urgency?"

She nodded. "You must drive me to town and we must be back before eight o'clock."

Queen O'Scots jumped to the top of the garden fence. Peggy escorted the interloper from the parameters of the police house and the cat observed every step. Miss Carstairs was already out of her cottage and striding towards them. Sir Roland, determined not to meet her, took to his heels and was gone, into the Twitchels and out to Back Lane, before the retired schoolma'am made it to the middle of The Street.

"Peggy! Come here!"

The old schoolma'am was all of a fluster. She had ran from her house without a headscarf and the buckles on her shoes were only half done up. "Whatever's the matter?" Peggy asked. She thought that a cup of tea might be in order, but Edna Carstairs was in no condition to hear talk of that sort.

"What are you doing with that ne'er do well? Keep away from him, do you hear!" She didn't realise how loud she was shouting. Maud Nevers opened her front door. Young Tommy Wheeler appeared at his bedroom window. "I've important news! Mavis Reynolds has just told me. Peggy, this is important. She saw Small Thin Annie talking to the vicar's maid."

Hearing her name rattling up The Street, little Annie quietly closed the lid on her money box and crept to her front door, where she knelt on the ginger bristled mat and listened through the letterbox.

"Edna, is there somewhere we can go?" Peggy was asking. "They were probably talking about Lipton's Tea wrappers."

"Oh Peggy, don't act the fool. Liptons is nothing to do with it. Mavis saw them talking."

"And Mavis heard every word?"

65

"You test my patience, young woman. Don't dare think that you're too old for a good telling off! They saw something. Small Thin Annie and the maid were looking out of the vicarage window and saw something in Miss Knightly's garden. You've got to investigate."

"Has it anything to do with dahlias?"

That stalled the old teacher. "Dahlias?" she queried, flummoxed. "I shouldn't think so."

Now, Nurse Everard was at Peggy's shoulder.

"Mrs. Pinch, I don't wish to interrupt you but Miss Anders is anxious for a little of your time. At once, I'm afraid. Expectations are limited."

Peggy felt the freeze of the Reaper's digging fingertip on the nape of her neck. She felt that the blue clouds at night were the cast of his palm over the village. He had taken Eliza Knightly with cruel malice aforethought and wouldn't move on until he had drawn those other waiting souls. It was his prospects that dampened the village spirits, kept folk indoors, forestalled too much talking and summoned all to their prayers.

"Two of us?" Edna offered.

But Peggy shook her head. "No, I don't think so. Not this time."

They had dismantled Poppy Anders' double bed, brought it downstairs and put it back together in her parlour. The foot-board pressed against the window ledge, the kitchen door opened behind Poppy's head and there was just enough room to step between the bedside and the fireplace.

She whispered to Peggy, "It will be easier for them to carry me out. They won't have to manage the stairs." She patted the paisley patterned eiderdown. "Sit down, Peggy. Our District Sow will be cutting us short before long and I need to explain my will."

"Never mind that." said Peggy, tucking the edge of the sheet more tidily around the old woman's throat. "How are you feeling?"

She was too exhausted to put any expression in her voice. "How am I feeling? Stupid child. I'm dying, that's how I'm feeling. Really, you get no better, Peggy Pinch. You always were an idle girl."

"And you've always kept an eye out for me," Peggy smiled and kissed the unmoving forehead.

The cough was pitifully weak. "My little joke," she explained. "How is the murder going?"

"You're not supposed to know about that."

"Nonsense. Of course, I know. Poor Eliza, she never deserved an end like that. She wouldn't have wished for chances to say good-bye, but she would have liked to make sure things were in order. 'Affairs', Peggy. One's affairs are very important in your last couple of days."

Nurse Everard was making a noise in the kitchen.

"She'll come in here and say it's time for my sleep. Doesn't she realise that I'll be sleeping for years on end? Now, Peggy, to business. My will."

"Tea for two," the nurse announced as she squeezed through the door and navigated her way around the bed. "A slice of bread and butter for the patient and a cheese scone for our caller. I've not heard of mustard with a scone before. I'm told it's a village curiosity." She set the tray on the window ledge within Peggy's reach. "Now, you make sure you have a good chat, Poppy. I don't want you falling asleep before you've said all that you want to say. Expectations are limited, my dear. Expectations are limited."

Poppy Anders did not wait for the tea to be poured. She nibbled at a corner of bread and butter and, when she was sure that the nurse was out of the way, she said, "I promised your mother that I would give you Laurel Cottage when I had finished with it. She knew that the day would come when you would lose the police house."

Peggy was lost for words.

"Now, my dear. There's bound to be a bit of a fuss. I have telephoned my best nephew and he has promised to explain things to the family. And our new Reverend is sure that I have left everything to him. Young fool. He needs to go into the army, that one." She lifted her head, an inch or two from her pillow. "You will tell him, won't you. Say, my little joke."

"Aunt Poppy, I'm so grateful. I don't know how to thank you."

"Now don't start that 'Aunt Poppy' lark. You'll get me thinking that we're both young again." She sighed and a life time of memories past though her mind. "It has been good," she said, very quietly. A tear was trickling down her cheek. "Expectations are rather limited, I'm afraid."

Peggy took her hand. Her fingers were cold and as brittle as twigs in winter. "Rest," she said. "Just for a while."

"Who gets Wayback Cottage?"

Peggy shook her head.

"They probably think that it passed to me and the two houses come as one package. Disappointed. They'll be disappointed." Then, the words 'Doctor Meriweather' hovered on her lips. She had been thinking aloud.

"Poppy, what about the doctor?"

But the old lady was half asleep and couldn't muster the words.

"Poppy, what did Miss Knightly tell you before she was killed?"

Peggy was sure that she smiled.

She encouraged the woman with a nod. "You called on her, the week before." The smile was still there but fading as she thought more and more about sleep. She opened her mouth a little and teased Peggy by touching her teeth with her tongue.

Peggy leant closer, putting an ear to the mouth

"Wouldn't you like to know," whispered the old lady and she managed a chuckle. "Meriweather knew that Wayback Cottage comes to me on Eliza's death. He saw her will. And he's been trying to get on my good side. You heard me, didn't you; he thinks he got a good chance of getting both houses as one package. I've let him think that, so they'll be a bit of a fuss. You will have to tell them all that wicked old Polly was having her little joke."

Chapter Five

Best Laid Plans

The empty bicycle lay in a ditch of weeds and stagnant water. It had been left against the five-bar gate but, unattended, had fallen back wheel first into the ditch and now looked abandoned. Pinch was not convinced that the bicycle was without personality and this constant falling over wasn't part of a petulant show. He sat on the other side of the lane, in the long grass of the embankment of Railway Bridge, Number Ninety-One. He had taken off his policeman's helmet and had placed it between his thighs so it could function as a tuck-box. He had chunks of ham with mustard from Florrie of Coutts Farm, two pears from the market orchard on the edge of Countess Whensbury's estate and a quart of honest home-brew from the back of the Bridge Tavern, three quarters of a mile away. Pinch did not consider himself a lazy copper, but he saw no excuse for avoiding those customs that had been in place for decades. Poachers left pairs of hares on his garden gate and lax licensees allowed him tasters of their peculiars.

He checked his pocket watch and belched. Sergeant Hawk was late. He fell to considering, not for the first time, the miserable condition of sheep. He had many times observed that there natural figure was with their heads and tails down. They moped, and small wonder. They lived a life without decision and were only useful when they were dead. It was a soporific debate and he next opened his eyes in response to the bulk that was his police sergeant establishing a seat in the grass at his side.

"Haven't got Number Twenty One, Number Thirty Three or Number Forty One have you?" asked Bernard Hawk.

"Monza, Sweden and Southport. That's all. Have you seen Number Twenty One?"

Hawk shook his head. "Not expecting it yet. They're holding back."

"So, just those cards and you've got the set? Well done."

"We need to talk about the current picture, Arthur."

"What picture?"

The sergeant picked at the packet of ham. "The whole picture. The situation."

"You're going to sack me." Pinch put on a grumbly face; his bottom lip went forward and his eyes peered sulkily from the shelter of his brow.

"Oh, hardly the sack, Arthur. Good lord, you're three years past the retirement age. No one can go on forever." Hawk interlocked his fingers over the top of his belly. He stretched his left leg which, gradually, pushed him to lying down. "These damned AA motorcycle patrols are the problem. The Chief has noticed how much ground they cover. Ideal for rural patches, he says."

"He's going to buy up the AA?" Pinch reasoned incredulously.

"No. He's talking about Bobbies on motorbikes covering three beats instead of one."

"You're going to sack me," Pinch repeated. The backs of his calves were aching and he wanted to stand up. He picked up a knob of cheese and dipped it in Florrie's mustard. "Gawd, I'd get to m'feet but for these damned knees. A chap's got to put a request in writing before they'll take any notice. They're like sheep, knees are. Have you ever thought it?"

"I've put forward a solution, Arthur. I've said it's nonsense to close a police house in a village so prone to murder. Great Scott, you've even got a German spy living in one of those thatched cottages."

"And the pilfering of school funds. Did you mention that?"

"And all those couples with young children."

Pinch drew breath through his closed teeth. "They'll never cope when the lads are fourteen," he said, shaking his head. "It's the public order we've got to account for."

"I've said, yes, Pinch should retire but be reinstated as a Special Constable, working hours as he can sensibly manage. On the cheap, you see."

"And the house?"

"For a peppercorn." He popped an olive in his mouth. "For as long as ye both shall live."

Pinch gave way. "I'm grateful, Bernard. Don't think that I'm not grateful." The call from a lonely sheep on the other side of the country lane seemed to reflect Pinch's resignation. "Miserable existence, you know, these sheep have."

"We've not got it agreed. There's the Watch Committee. There's always the Watch Committee."

"That bugger Templar's the stickler. That family's been on the Committee for too long."

"Generations," Bernard Hawk agreed.

Pinch lazily scanned the horizon. "My Peggy is up to something. He's got her riled. That's how I'd put it."

"Oh dear. Peggy Pinch riled and unforgiving." He shook his head. "Not a prospect to ponder over." Hawk eyed the empty beaker of ale. "Where'd you get the beer from?"

"The Bridge. Go round the back and they'll look after you, just fine. The Bridge likes to have a Bobby in her kitchen. But I can't join you, Skipper, I have some business to do at the Bad Bull on my way back."

Sergeant Hawk laughed. "You'll get no ale on the house there. 'Hate 'em all.' That's the BB's approach to the police, corn-wigged lawyers and the Revenue Men." He took a pocket watch from the breast of his tunic. "I need to get back to town. You're a good copper, Arthur. Long in the tooth and sour in condition, but a sound copper all the same."

The Bad Bull, on the edge of Pinch's beat, was a country pub well known for its suffocating warmth and its narrow 'take it or leave it' choice of ales. Folk spoke of 'smelling of the BB' meaning a mix of log smoke, spilt beer and myrtle. A long haired Afghan hound mooched from favourite place to favourite place. A yellowing photograph of a haughty Queen Mary was pinned next to the clock behind the bar. Facilities included a dart board and a skittle run on rugged boards. It was the last pub in the area to play a bespoke version of cribbage, retaining some of the terminology of the Tudor 'noddy' card game. A shove halfpenny board was kept behind the bar and issued only on orderly nights because of a brawl in 1926.

The publican wore a variety of coloured striped shirts and gypsy braces and usually worked with a tea towel slung over one shoulder. "Evening, Harfa," he called, alerting all to a policeman's presence. He pulled half a pint of mild ale and set it on the counter. "A nicely settled evening. Beating the bounds, are you?"

A loud voice shouted from the far end, "Another half mile and we'd be none of your business, Harfa." This was Barnaby, a well muscled carter from town. Pinch expected him to be trouble. This was going to be a twitchy half hour.

He sipped the top of his mild and asked quietly, "Have you got a lock-in tonight?"

"Just four of the lads, Harfa. I'll be hosting them for less than an hour. Forty minutes and they've usually done."

"I'll have a word with them perhaps." He had spotted the humble quartet in a nook of their own, away from the front door. Cheap tobacco smoke hung over their table like blue Wills o'the Wisp.

"A nip in your ear," he said and placed his tankard in the middle of the oak table. "I've got wind of your practical jokes." He paused for the announcement to have its effect. "You've had your fun. Tonight's the night to call it off."

He sensed Barnaby's approach. "These boys here are doing no harm. You leave them be."

"If I've picked up word of what's going on, it'll be common talk before long."

"Harfa, we're all pals in this house, aren't we?" said the long-haired farm hand in the corner. "Someone get Harfa a chair."

Pinch pressed on. "Now Albert, how would things go if your Elsie found her way into tonight's lock-in."

"Ah, Constable Pinch, that's hardly playing the game."

The youngest of them put in, "I wouldn't want my Jelly to hear of it."

"We accept your challenge, don't we lads?" laughed Barnaby, moving to within an inch of Pinch's shoulder and pushing his belly forward. "We'll get twice as fly and you try to catch us out."

"No, I'm out of it," Albert declared. "Harfa's right. If he knows about the sport, it'll be broad knowledge afore long."

"You're right, Albie. I can't have the pranks reaching my Jelly's ears."

Pinch counted four against one. He saw no advantage in seeking unqualified capitulation, so he withdrew to the bar and drank alone.

The landlord said over his shoulder, "I'll see there's no silliness." They both understood, as Barnaby would have been quick to remind them, that if Pinch ever snitched on after hours drinking, he would have found his work impossible in the district. Compromise was in the murky air of the Bad Bull that night.

He ordered a second ale to show that he could not be intimidated. "What's the talk about our murder?" he asked.

The barman waited until he had done polishing a glass, then leaned over the counter as if he was about to share a confidence. "Favourite story is that someone was brought in from the outside to do it and get away with it. Complicated, that woman. She had complicated circumstances."

The Gaumont picture house, just three minutes walk through the back streets from the solicitors' office, was cold, damp, and dark and any talking had to be done in whispers. This was not the nicest of the town's cinemas. Every thing from the paper tickets to the typed list of rules not to be broken was curled at the corners. Neither families nor courting couples came to the

Gaumont. The lovers who found refuge in its darkened space were of a shiftier class. When the show started at half past six, George Templar and his secretary had been in their seats for fifteen minutes. And they had been waiting in the shady foyer for twenty before that, since George thought they were safer here than working late in the office.

Images flickered on the screen and lips moved out of time with their words. But neither mattered. Prim Miss Twinn had decided not to wear spectacles and could see none of the pictures on the screen.

"Oh, I do like an Edgar Wallace, don't you, Georgie?"

He laid his hand over hers on their shared armrest. "Very much, dear."

"It's said there's a mysterious room and a hand comes out from a hidden cupboard. Oh, Georgie, just imagine it for real." She pressed herself against his arm and moved her head as if she wanted to tuck it into the lap of his shoulder. Perhaps she wanted to lay it upon his beating breast.

Templar moved his hand from the armrest to the private portion of her dress. It stayed there, palm upwards, fingers curled and knuckles pressing so slightly down. Immediately, her throat went dry, her pulse quickened and, though she couldn't tell, her skin flushed red from her neck to the top of her cleavage.

"Oh Georgie, it's lovely being alone."

"Hardly alone, Dorothy dear. But we can enjoy an hour and a half, simply being together."

The Gaumont was less than half full. Templar and Twinn were seated in the back row of the stalls and could count the backs of twenty four heads, mostly in ones, sometimes in twos but never in threes.

"I don't like that Peggy Pinch," whispered Twinn. "She has a naughty look about her."

Templar's long fingers, walnut coloured and as scrawny as a poor widow's sausage, flexed in her lap, so slowly that they could hardly be noticed.

Miss Twinn looked up to his face and breathed, "Oh, Georgie. Let's go back early to the office. Neither of us really want to watch the silly film. Go back now and we'll have even longer together. Properly together, I mean."

Lights out, blinds down, sweet Lettice Templar made the tiniest crack at the window and looked down on The Street below. "He's parked up the Square, waiting," she reported.

Peggy Pinch, who was on her knees and working in the excuse-me room, reminded her that Sir Roland was not due to be at the end of the alley until ten minutes past seven. She checked her watch and went on working.

The toilet tissue stretched from the pedestal and half way along the first floor landing. Jamie had stressed that the powder should be dusted as faintly as possible. Imagine that it needs air to breathe, he had said. "If you blob it in bumps, the grains can't work up their mischief."

"Are you sure this will work?" asked Lettice, walking idly around her husband's office.

"If it doesn't, we'll try something else."

"Oh, my God!" gasped Lettice. Heavy footsteps on the pavement approached the front door. A gloved hand rattled the door handle.

"Oh, my God!" she said again. She had scurried to the top of the stairs and, saw the outline of a figure through the pebbled glass of the door. "It's the policeman. Peggy, the police."

Peggy estimated that she had laid a trail of itching powder, fifteen feet long. Now she needed to complete a professional job of returning it to the toilet roll so that no one would suspect it had been tampered with. "He's checking that the premises are secure," she explained calmly. "The beat man is supposed to do it at six o'clock and ten o'clock. That's why I told Sir Roland to keep out of sight before seven. Now, please, Lettice. Don't tread on anything. Just stay there. This is the important bit."

"Cor, those drains are strong. You've not tampered with them, have you?"

"Lettice, of course not. Now, let me get on."

The wronged wife sat on the top step and sighed. "I wonder what they're up to. Do you think they are kissing? I mean, right now. I don't mind if they are. Really, I don't. But I've got to tell them I know."

"Yes, well," said Peggy, bringing her paraphernalia together. "We've left a nice message to let them know. It's time to leave."

"I'll just use the cloakroom."

"You can't." Peggy was amazed. How could her accomplice be so simple? "I've doctored the paper. You can't ..." She shook her head. "You can't use the paper."

"Got to go," Lettice giggled, bobbing on her feet like a mischievous sixteen year old. "I'll tell you what." She pushed past Peggy and, nipping into her husband's office, returned with a handkerchief from his raincoat pocket. "He'll never know," she said.

Lettice would have been content to leave the toilet door open, but Peggy pulled it closed and waited. She was worried about the time. She had checked when the Gaumont's first house closed and knew that the lovers would return to their nest before long. "There we are," Lettice announced when she reappeared. "I've kept it as clean as I could."

"Here," said Peggy taking hold of the hanky. "Go downstairs and be ready to leave by the scullery door." She brought the last of the itching powder from her waistband and carefully spilled it into the handkerchief. She ruffled it, then pushed it deep into the coat pocket, hanging on the hook behind the office door.

As soon as she walked into the kitchen, she knew that something had gone wrong. The back door was open, Lettice had gone but there was no sound of her footsteps in the side alley. Peggy crept forward. She poked her nose into the cold of the night air. Lettice had pressed herself hard against the brick wall. She signalled that Peggy should not make a sound.

"It's your sergeant," she whispered.

Sure enough, the grey shape of the policeman was blocking their exit to the street. His back was turned, he was standing at ease and going up and down on the balls of his feet, like policemen do.

Chapter Six

An Incident After Dark

Peggy took the keys from Lettice's frozen fingers and locked the doors. At least, they were no longer burglars.

"No, I wouldn't, sir," the sergeant was saying. "Not down the alley, sir. Not tonight."

Templar's worthless, crow-like face came into view. Peggy and Lettice tried to merge their little figures into the brickwork. In a bedroom, next door, someone had turned their wireless on. Peggy heard the gruff uncertain voice of Ramsey MacDonald speaking to the nation. There was more fizz and crackle than oratory.

"Sergeant Hawk," the solicitor was saying with feigned patience. "You know very well that I work in these offices."

"I do, sir. But not tonight, sir. Not down the alley. We've had an unfortunate report."

"Unfortunate? Really, I must say this is intolerable."

"An exhibitionist." The Sergeant kept his military stance. His hands held loosely behind his back and his feet apart. Up and down he went, as if he were keeping time.

"Exhibitionist? Sergeant, I'll put up with an exhibition."

Hawk looked straight ahead. "The gentleman in question, sir, has an intent to insult a female."

"An intent to … oh my Goodness." Templar stumbled over the words. "But he won't come out while you're standing there, surely?"

"It'll worry him. It does the sort no harm to be a little anxious. I dare say that the gentleman will be in tears when he does come out."

The solicitor nodded. "We'll use the front door."

"We? I didn't know you weren't alone."

Miss Twinn stepped out of the shadows.

"Oh, I see," said the sergeant.

Templar was rattled. "No, sergeant. I don't think you see at all."

"You've read my proposal?"

"What rot are you talking about?" Templar glanced at his lover, then back to Hawk. "Yes, of course. Your ideas for Mr Pinch. You understand that these matters are usually left in the hands of the Chief Constable but I am sure the Watch Committee will raise no objection. Probably, a cautionary remark. Just for the minutes. Good night, Sergeant Hawk." He stepped back, nodded at Miss Twinn and stepped to the front door of the terraced office.

Hawk waited for half a minute more than was necessary before moving to the centre of the pavement where he turned and lifted his finger to the peak of his helmet in a modest salute as Peggy moved into the light. The coast was clear.

Their footsteps echoed down the street as they ran into the open pavement. With no good-byes, Lettice ran across the road, down an alley and into the side door of the Talbot Tavern. That disappearing figure in a pink and crimson coat was the last that Peggy would see of her. Hawk had discreetly and silently moved out of view and Peggy had to dither for no more than a couple of seconds before Sir Roland's automobile paused at the kerb and Peggy dived in.

"Successful?" he asked, steering his way through the Market Place towards the open road.

"Successful, I think so. A little bit nervy but really, it was all rather clever." Of course, she was cold, short of breath and sorely in need of a cloakroom but: "It was all so beautiful in a way. Like a work of art. I can't expect others to understand." She thought, did girls at boarding school feel like this when they have worked a prank against their prefects?

This was not Peggy's first ride in a motorcar - she had been frequently ferried in constabulary vehicles between village and town - but never before had she been carried through the night or driven so fast. She was bumped and rattled and she was cold but, more than that, she was thrilled. Sir Roland mistook her feminine fidgeting for anxiety and said, loud above the engine, "Don't worry. I'll not touch you."

Why did he need to say that?

The hedges and verges flew through the beam of the headlamps so quickly that Peggy was unable to identify them. It wasn't long before Peggy Pinch didn't know where she was. Only gradually did she become aware that she had engineered a precarious situation for herself. Not only was she alone with a man, in the dark and in the middle of nowhere, but he was in control of anything that might happen. And, whatever happened, she would be blamed for being so flighty, so flirty some might say, in making herself so vulnerable. She may feel smug about putting herself 'one-up' on the solicitor and that awful Twinn woman, but now she was being driven fast through an escapade which could not turn out well.

Instinctively, she tried to make herself skimpier. Her breathing, never expressive, shallowed and she resolved to say nothing. If she asked him to stop the car, saying that she would walk the rest of the way, she was sure that she wouldn't be long in the dark before she was offered a lift by another passing motorist. But how would she explain things? How had she allowed herself to get into such a risky situation? She tried to pick up clues from the look on his face but there were no street lamps and no lights from houses, and when tiny bulbs on his controls occasionally flickered, their reflections brought forward a purple or mauve face which seem to emerge disembodied in the blackness.

"The man's deceit makes me wild. He didn't tell you that he wasn't the driver? Yes, the Spider crossed the finishing line in less than forty-five seconds but Templar wasn't at the wheel. Wistow's our whizz-oh wheeler by far. She barks like a machine gun - that's the twin cylinders. I promise you, nothing could touch her on the hills in the twenties. Of course, she's nearly ten years old, 'though they've re-thought the brakes, and it takes a racing demon like Farmer Wistow to get the most out of her."

"Our farmer drives racing motorcars?" Peggy asked uncertainly.

"He's ace!"

She thought that Sir Roland spoke like a child.

He eagerly worked the rudimentary pedals and levers, leaning forward over the steering wheel. When the excitement discomforted him, his left hand went to the crotch of his trousers and sometimes dallied there.

She turned her face to the side window.

"Please, you mustn't worry. I won't touch you."

There, he'd said it again.

"I want to show you something, then Mr Pinch and the others must decide what to do about it. I've decided that its time for the truth to come out. My father insisted that I should keep the secret safe, like he had done, so that the family may be protected. But who am I protecting? No family is left except me, alone. So, I've decided."

The car had reached the bottom of Back Lane where Sir Roland drew up some fifty yards short of the Hall. He switched off the engine and extinguished the old fashioned motoring lamps. He said, "The Templars and Byriver Hall are like feuding families in a three volume novel."

"You mean, since the old Victorian murder?"

"But the Templars provoked that murder. They gave my great-grandfather no choice but to kill another of the family. A horrible thing to do. They called the two brothers to their chambers and invited one to accuse the other of stealing from the church."

"And was the accusation sound?"

"What do you think of the place? Isn't it a monstrosity? Byrivers isn't really a hall, not even a manor house, it's a nightmare put together by a feted soldier over a hundred years ago. My grandfather's great uncle. We've all had to live in it ever since, like prisoners shackled to the past. I used to pretend that it was Abbotsford, harbouring the ghosts of Rob Roy and Ivanhoe. You don't mind me talking, do you?"

"I'd rather be on my way, Roland. I can walk safely from here."

"No. Please, stay." She sensed a change in his voice, a threat that he would not allow this night to slip through his fingers. "I've something I want to show you," he said again. She prayed to God that he would stop saying it. "Only, I wanted to explain about the house first. I won't take long. My father's bedroom had a balcony and I'd get on it and pretend it was the battlements. You see, I couldn't get away from the sense that the whole building was somehow tied up in the past."

She took hold of the door lever. "Sir Roland, I am going to say goodnight."

"No, you mustn't. It's taken a lot of nerve to say what I've said and I want to finish. The house has ghosts. And witches. And sometimes the witches can get the better of you. Of me, I mean."

A motorcycle spluttered as it turned at the top of Back Lane and, after a moment's hesitation, the rider began his ride down the road, towards them. His cycle chain rattled. The lone headlamp made long shadows of the trees and, as it past Colonel Hatchett's ostentatious residence, Peggy caught sight of his manservant watching from the staircase window. The beam from the headlamp swept this way and that as the cyclist unsteadily manoeuvred his handlebars. Peggy could not tell how far away he was but, without warning, the car's interior was lit up.

She screamed, both hands going to her mouth; Sir Roland had been sitting with his trousers fully undone.

Peggy leaned against the door and fell backwards, her shoulder bouncing on the grass bank as she rolled over. She started shouting, stupidly, and forced herself into a run. She didn't care where her feet were treading or how much the bushes and trees scratched her arms. She had fled for several seconds before she realised that she had ran into the Twitchels. She stopped to get her bearings; lights from bedroom windows along The Street were at her back. She was perhaps a hundred yards from the boundary with Wretched Lane. Thinking, 'don't stop, don't stop' in time with her panting, she hid herself in the bushes and listened. Something was trying to creep into her shoe. She closed her eyes tight. Mouse or shrew, she didn't want to see it. With a hand against a low branch that swayed too easily, she leaned sideways and made sure that nothing was hiding in her foot.

The motorcycle had got as far as the track that ran along the brookside at the bottom of the village. He had dowsed the headlamp but managed to keep the engine running and he manhandled the machine into the bottom reaches of the Twitchels. He progressed slowly in the dark, his wheels slipping on the stony bumps and treacherously muddy ruts. A few minutes of this and the motor died. Peggy thought that he had stopped and was listening for anyone moving in the thickets. Once or twice, she heard him push the motorbike through branches and undergrowth, but one moment he was to her left and the next to the right. He was getting near. No, he was further away.

As her confidence steadied, Peggy realised that she could not remain hidden until morning. She stepped forward.

The Reverend Sullivan, astride the saddle, was unbuttoning the strap of his helmet, revealing his face with its goatie beard and the slick of curled hair. "My Gosh," he said, wiping a forelock of the black hair from his face. "Yes. Gosh, it's Mrs. Pinch and I'm glad I've caught you because I need to make amends."

Peggy realised that he had no idea that anything had happened in Back Lane. She said, "Really, vicar? I doubt that very much," but was unable to clear the puzzled look from her face. It was as if an unexpected conversation between the trees in the middle of the night was no more than a casual occurrence.

"No, I do. I do. I was absent when your husband and our doctor were coping with poor Eliza's death. The village was in turmoil while I caught up with other things. It was just for a moment but I feel terribly bad about it."

"You were helping with Poppy's trunk call."

"Yes. Quite right. I went across at a five and twenty past two and didn't get away until - well, after six o'clock. It wasn't just making the call, though that turned out to be far more complicated than we were led to believe, but it was preparing Miss Anders beforehand, and helping her through all the upset afterwards. It was hardly the sort of thing that a vicar could leave half cooked. You must remember, I didn't know that poor Eliza was dead. Not at the start."

"Everyone understands, vicar. You work terribly hard."

"No, I should have called at the police house in the evening and thanked Constable Pinch for all his sterling work but ..."

Peggy nodded. "You were exhausted. vicar, you are working too hard. You can't see things that are right in front of you."

"I do feel like that, sometimes. It makes me wonder if I'm any use at all." He frowned. "Was anything untoward, just now? At first, I thought you were running away."

"Not at all."

"I say, he wasn't up to anything improper, was he? I beg your pardon, Mrs. Pinch."

What was he thinking now? What was all this 'begging your pardon' nonsense?

"Did he touch you? You must say."

"No, not at all." She buried her face in her hands. "It was my fault. I shouldn't have allowed myself to get into that situation. I've been stupid, stupid, stupid. But, thanks to you, very lucky. Please, you mustn't tell anyone what's happened."

"Of course not. If you want me to stay quiet, I shall say not a word."

"I couldn't bear any talk. Oh, Lord, I feel like a loose woman."

"Well, you mustn't. A lady is entitled to expect protection and good manners when she is alone with a gentleman. What's that you've got?"

"Nothing except some litter that got pushed into my shoe." She tilted the little tickets of card until they caught some light from a bedroom. "Numbers Fifteen and Eighteen, but they're very muddy."

He chuckled. "Oggie cards. They're everywhere, even at times like this. Now, I think it would be best if I walked you home." He added, "At least, to the edge of The Street."

Peggy nodded. "I must say, I'd be grateful for the light from your headlamp."

"Rest assured, I shall catch the scoundrel and put him straight."

Mistress Reynolds, ready for bed and holding her candlewick dressing gown together as she drew her curtains, watched them walk - as slowly as lovers, she thought - into the bushes and beyond to the grass verge of The Street. There, a safe distance from the police house, they appeared to say goodnight without touching. She was sure that they had already shared their goodnight kiss.

She placed the oatmeal drink and a home baked biscuit at her bedside and confided with Marmaduke as she encouraged him to settle on his patch of her eiderdown at the foot of the bed. She started to click her tongue against her front teeth, a habit for which Maud Nevers was always telling her off. The policeman's wife went stumbling and tripping through life, always in error but always, it seemed to Mistress Reynolds, able to get away with her silliness. Now - oh, now, how delicious - she had gone too far. With one snap of her fingers - and that is what the woman did - Miss Mavis Reynolds of Dublin Cottage could spring the trap of come-uppance. "Poor Peggy Pinch," (Even the tabby Marmaduke could sense no sincerity in that whisper of sympathy.) "She cannot know what we know about his Reverence, can she? Marmaduke, we shall conspire. We shall set the hares running and that Peggy will learn what a jealous rival mealy Polly Adam can be. And when we're ready, we'll start the tongues a-wagging."

The cat mewed and leaped from the bed

"What's this? You can't want more milk. Or is it the outside night you want? You want to go and work your mischief. You have spells to weave and cat's paths to lay that no-one can cross without misfortune. Why, yes. You must."

She slipped from her sheets, took up the cat in one elbow as she opened the bedroom window with her other hand. "Of course, you must do your mistress's bidding." With a force that took the cat by surprise, she threw the feline into the blackness of the night.

Chapter Seven

P.C. and Mrs. Pinch in Progress

When the church clock struck eleven, it seemed that wicked goblins had sent a last chime missing. The evening had a creepy midnight feel. No one mentioned that a murderer was in their midst and, for another night, the police house seemed no nearer making an arrest. Only innocent children slept soundly. Jamie Eider, engrossed in his pharmacy, was late in and escaped a telling off by climbing the staircase, taking off his clothes and going into bed without a word. He dozed and opened his eyes when his father stood at the foot of the bed reading the fifth commandment from the scripture. Those grown-ups who sat up on puffed up pillows, reluctant to extinguish their bedside lamps, were those with something to hide in their hearts. Unbeknown to one another, many prayed that night, coincidentally several at the same time: 'if I should die before I wake, I pray the Lord my soul will take.'

Gort's dog barked.

As Peggy approached the police house, she tried to keep her shoes as quiet as she could on the roadside grit. Queen O'Scots was seated to attention on the parapet of Edna's gatepost and Peggy heard a crack, far off, as a poacher had a go at one of the local pheasants. Blue clouds passed over the moon. Now and then, she saw the flicker of a bicycle lamp as it bobbled along Back Lane.

Her parlour lights were on and, through the bow window, she could see Doctor Meriweather in his overcoat and scarf, standing in the middle of the carpet, talking down to Arthur. It wasn't a wife's place to interrupt her husband's conversation with a local gentleman, so she crept along the side path and through the back door to the scullery. She had her hat and coat off before her breathing settled down. She weighed the water in the kettle and set it on the heat. There was so much that she needed to get out of her head before she spoke with Arthur. Now, scones and jam. Where were Edna's scones?

Meriweather was saying, "I feel that I've not been fair with you, Pinch, so I've come to set things right between us."

"Help yourself to a bowl of tobacco. It's Bishop's Move."

"No, I don't usually smoke this late."

"Oh, come-come. Is it bad manners for two men to share the sociability of a pipeful?"

"I want to explain. I didn't take the blood sample when you were there. I waited until you had gone, but that's because I didn't think it necessary at first." He had expected some reaction but, of course, Arthur Pinch stayed his counsel. "You remarked on her crossed feet."

"Uneasy, they were."

"And I said she had probably fallen into the chair. But later, I thought that she might have struggled to stand up and that's unusual in heart failure. Folk feel like they'll recover if they stay still."

"So you went back into the house?"

Meriweather was standing still but he had taken off his cap and he was fumbling it between two hands. "Almost immediately.

The important point is that I heard somebody walking around upstairs."

"The important point? Apart from the poison in the blood, you mean?"

"Quite. Yes - I see what you mean. Naphthalene poisoning. We are supposed to be more careful these days but it's easily enough found in old stocks of moth balls. Death is usually very unpleasant but, intravenously, it would quicken the heart rate almost immediately. Miss Knightly had no chance of fighting it, I'm afraid."

He had taken to rubbing the lining of his cap between his thumb and forefinger, like an infant's comforter. "I wondered if it was Sullivan," he broached hesitantly.

"Unlikely," remarked Pinch. "He was in Laurel Cottage with Poppy Anders."

"Yes, that's what I've heard, but the man has come to our village under a cloud."

"That's loose talk," Pinch interrupted. "I've heard as much as you have."

"His bishop has no high opinion of him. He was dispatched to our village as a sanction. We are his last chance. "

Without taking Sullivan's side, Pinch tried to inject some balance. He said, "A word's been put in my ear, Meriweather. Bishop Vaughan disparages many young men who have been through St Johns. It's an independent seminary that takes boys who can't manage university."

"But there has to be more to it."

"I shouldn't think so. "

"He's said that he doesn't like parish work," the doctor persisted.

"It's all balls."

Peggy, listening from inside her pantry, put her fingertips to her mouth in surprise. She had not heard her husband use the term before indoors, although things fruity were called to aid in the garden sometimes.

"Where's the vicar who doesn't like parish work?" Pinch argued. "It's why they've become vicars."

"He wanted a specialist ministry, away from people. They spoke to him about the army, but he wouldn't take it because he'd have to mess with the men."

"Doctor, doesn't this all sound like nasty talk? And we'd do well to keep it battened down."

It was five and twenty to twelve, well past the Pinches' bedtime. The wireless programmes had finished for the evening and Pinch had lodged a last log in the fire grate. He was wearing his old corduroys with three fly buttons missing. "I don't like the man," he muttered. "He wouldn't share a pipe with me. It'd be a mistake to trust him, Mrs. Pinch."

When it was clear that Pinch wasn't thinking of going up, she set about darning toes and heels by the light of a paraffin lamp.

"Did he make love to you?" he asked moderately; he wasn't looking for trouble but he sensed that things had gone wrong.

"Certainly not. He was trying to work out how much we've learned about the murder. He's rather a silly man, Arthur. He proceeded with a sense of theatre which made him look foolish. Very foolish. However, never mind the melodrama, he told a story which goes along the lines of another yarn from Templar's."

"It's some five and fifty years old, Mrs. Pinch, his family's history of murder and stolen church treasure. No, no, no." The policeman nibbled the tip of his pipe stem with two front teeth. "No, there are three matters in these circumstances that weigh heavier than others do." Then he fell quiet as he again rehearsed the discrepancies in his mind. The pear log settled between the old coals, producing a warm cosiness, homely and closed in, scented with the unique strains which made up the Pinches and their household.

"First, there is the matter of the racing car at the Bottom."

Peggy nodded, carefully protecting her fingertips as she stitched. "It belongs to the solicitor, Templar. He admits driving it."

"But no-one heard him drive through the ford."

Pinch went on nibbling.

"Would you like a whiskey, dear?" she asked.

"Yes. A good idea, thank you, and pour something for yourself."

Peggy set her needlework aside and went off to the kitchen. Left alone, Pinch thought aloud: "Footsteps upstairs are no surprise. It would have been remarkable if there had been no footsteps."

"Did you know that Farmer Wistow drives racing cars?" she called through. "Sir Roland says he's whizzo!"

She shouted, "Stop! Queenie, come here!" The cat had got between her legs as she carried a bold tumbler of Scotch and, for herself, a glass of Miss Carstairs' pears and peach and very light sherry.

"No, no. She's fine." Pinch, whose friendship with the schooma'am's cat was of longer standing than most people

94

realised, emitted a low and croaky groan, not unlike a purr, as the pet curled herself between the turn-ups of his old trousers.

Peggy offered the obvious solution. "He took the unsuitable way to Marston Westerley, but why on earth?"

"He wouldn't have got all the way, not in that brute of a motor. French, wasn't it? Or German. The German's make motors that are way bigger than they ought to be. "

She was ready to say that Sir Roland was sure it was English but thought it unnecessary to be too wise too often. "To meet someone, perhaps," Peggy suggested as she reorganised the next twenty minutes of darning.

Pinch leaned forward, brought the tobacco caddy to his lap and went through the thumb and finger ritual of recharging his pipe. It appeared to be more complicated than it should have been, yet carried out with such dexterity that no other way could match it. Even Queen O'Scots turned her head.

"Second, there is the matter of the late night walk in carpet slippers," he said, turning the bowl of the pipe in his hand. "I've retraced her steps with Jacoby and, d'you know Peggy, I've a notion that Spinster Knightly was peeking on Mavis Reynolds, the night before she was murdered."

"Mavis Reynolds? But Arthur, why?"

"She has worked as a nurse, hasn't she?"

Peggy replied, "During the war, yes. But, no, she wouldn't have been trained to give injections."

"Not properly, at least," said Pinch, very quietly. "And finally, the matter of the cancelled visit."

"No, not finally. Pinch, what was Prim Miss Twinn doing in our church?"

"There can't be anything wrong in that," her husband remarked. By now, he was deep into his pipe and Queen O'Scots seemed settled for the night.

"I walked up the Waddie to the vicarage," Peggy explained. "You know, you get a good view of the churchyard path before anyone there can see you. That's when I saw the new vicar's maid hurrying back from the church, all of a dither."

"Did you ask her why?"

"Bless, Pinch, no. That's between her and her maker. But I did peek inside the church, just to see who had upset her."

"Miss Prim-Twinn? Peg, people pray for quite innocent reasons. They don't necessarily have a guilty conscience."

"But why our church? She could kneel before any number of alters in town."

Pinch wrapped a thumb and forefinger around his chin. "I get what you're thinking. Some long-standing friendship with our new vicar? We'll leave that piece of the jigsaw on the table for later. We cannot put off the cancelled visit any further; what do you make of it?"

"I want to talk about that, Pinch; it makes no sense. It's all a show. We know one thing. Miss Knightly had asked Templars to undertake an inventory. That suggests that she had recently changed her will."

Pinch nodded. "Templar could give us the details."

"Then, we are told, she cancelled the appointment." Peggy shook her head decisively. "Miss Twinn took the phone call and assumed it was Miss Knightly but it may not have been. That's nonsense. She would have recognised any imposter. She made a mistake. She wanted to add some colour to her account so she said that Miss Knightly was busy cultivating dahlias. But Miss

Knightly was adverse to those flowers and, certainly, none are growing in her garden."

"So, Miss Twinn took a step too far," Pinch remarked, adding, "Compelling," with greater mystery than he intended.

Peggy continued. "Still, Miss Knightly prepares the sandwiches and, still, Templar drives to the village. But that's exactly how things would have happened if no phone call had been made. The appointment is made, the sandwiches laid out and Templar arrives."

"But his client is dead by that time, so he drives on."

"He has no idea where to go and runs out of the road on the way to Marston Westerley."

Pinch gave up nibbling and reached for his tobacco.

He was thinking of his conversation with Jacoby. "Evidence is the problem. We work in a system that relies on evidence but Johnny Murderer is in charge of the evidence. He decides what evidence is left behind, to fool us, and the evidence we never find."

Peggy laid her darning in her lap. She wanted to sit closer to him, at his feet perhaps but she knew that his mood was tentative. He was ready to close the conversation and withdraw with little provocation. She said, "The Liverpool murder. You think so much about it, Pinch. It's changed the way you feel about policing."

He conceded a little, a bit of a nod to one side. "Not my level of policing. I am here to help the village keep on an even keel. That won't change. But the detectives will never control crime while they have to rely on evidence."

"Heaven forbid, we should ever be guided by anything other than evidence."

He was trying to keep any excitement from his voice. In truth, he felt some passion for the subject but allowing it to show would give too much of himself away. "One day," he began, before coughing. "Science will catch up and provide a thread of evidence, so proven, that no-one will be able to dispute it. We thought we were there with fingerprints but Johnny Murderer learned to wear gloves. But you're right about the Liverpool job. Everyone asks, was Wallace guilty when of course he wasn't. And that's not the point. The point ..." He looked across the hearth. "You've stopped your needlework."

"The point, yes?"

"That Johnny Murderer, whoever he is, was able to divert the boys from any evidence that might identify him. The point is that circumstances are in his favour and ..." He looked around for his gardening book. "... he's better than us."

"Is it time we went up?"

He got to his feet and stood on the hearthrug, drawing heavily on his pipe. "Peggy, do you think that you could get closer to Templar. He might, I'm not sure, give something away?"

"It would be easier if there was something definite that I needed to discover."

"Oh, yes. Of course."

She said, to encourage him, "You want me to flirt?"

"It's his Achilles heel." He looked at her, face to face. "Forget it. I was carried away. Too much thinking. Nothing good ever comes of it."

All had gone wrong in the cold and damp office of George Templar.

"I'm burning!" His lover, naked from the waist down, pranced around the tacky carpet, rubbing her bottom with both hands and pressing her buttocks together. "It's your fault."

Templar had withdrawn to the safety of his desk. "How can it be my fault?" He crouched down to pull up his trousers.

"You've infected me! God, there is no one else. You've got the pox, you filthy rabbit."

"How come?"

Miss Twinn, her slender legs turning red, flew to the open doorframe. She pulled her bottom apart so that she could rub it vigorously on a corner of the poorly painted wood. Up and down. Up and down. This way and that. "Christ, they're swelling up," she yelled when she caught sight of her thighs. "My arse is on fire!"

He tried to argue reasonably. "Angel, please. People will hear on the street."

But Miss Twinn had lost all control of her cries. "Oh My God!" She pulled at her front, yanking her breasts from their bra and immediately scratching them with the ferocity of a wretched dog digging up a bone. "Help me. George, for God's sake scratch them."

He approached her and offered his hands.

"Oh God! You're useless." Her slap to the side of his jaw sent him rolling back to his desk. "Look at me! Pox ridden and rotting. I shall get my own back!" she yelled. "I shall tell how you murdered that woman!"

At two in the morning, lying quite still and looking up at the ceiling, Peggy Pinch complained, "What has the King got to do with it?"

Her husband grunted. He was awake but wouldn't admit it.

"MacDonald said that the King had asked him to form a government. It's nothing to do with him. There should be an election."

"There will be. This lot won't last long." Pinch struggled to sit up in the bed, a panting, gasping movement which resembled a hippopotamus trying to bend itself double. "It's not the King, it's the Crown. Peggy, I've explained all this to you."

"And when there's an election, his vote will count the same as mine."

"I'm not sure the King is allowed to take part," said Pinch patiently. "He has a role. A thingy role."

"Constitutional."

"I been through it with you." He swung his feet to the chilly floor. He was hungry. He knew that cold ham was on the marble slab in the larder. It would go nicely with a dash of coarse mustard. He sniffed and wiped his nose on the back of his hand.

Peggy kept her stare on the ceiling. "What does 'intent to insult a female' mean?"

Arthur Pinch did not answer for three or four seconds. "Is that it? Has that bugger been showing himself off to you?"

"I'm not sure. I mean, not actually."

"It means that he's stiff and standing to attention."

"I only saw it for a moment. A lady wouldn't look for longer than she had."

"A lady, perhaps not. But I know my Peggy Pinch. She'd take a darned good look."

"Don't mention it, Pinch. Not to anyone. Not even to him. Lord, I couldn't stand it if people got to hear. I'd rather you belt me for being so stupid." The broad leather strap with its brass buckle had not been taken out of the bottom drawer of the landing chest for years. For a moment, no more, her suggestion brought a rareness to the smoky living room.

Pinch made nothing of it. He asked, "Where did it happen? In town, in that car of his, in Byriver House?"

Peggy let her head fall to one side. He was still sitting on the edge of the bed with his back to her. She asked quietly, "Does it make a difference?"

"We can't have that sort of thing happening in the village. It's my job to put a stop to it."

"Oh, please Pinch, no. I just couldn't bear it."

"In my own way, dear. 'Ways and means'. A Bobby's first port of call. Ways and means. I'll put a stop to it in my own way."

"I can't be sure. See, he's very small and I think he was stiff but it loped to one side."

He clapped his hands on the knees of his candy striped pyjamas. "Shall we go downstairs for a pot of tea?"

Unusually, Pinch went to the front door of the police house and, leaving the door open, smoked his pipe on the front porch. He always thought that his troubled village recovered itself in the night. No other soul was out of bed. The cats and dogs, weasels and stoats, having feasted on their midnight prey, had withdrawn to their favourite shelters and watched. The stray mongrel had given up on the vicarage and, for two nights, had weighed the prospects of Cart and Gort. A lantern burned all night above the step of Laurel Cottage and Miss Nevers, who slept downstairs, had opened her curtains when she was sure that everyone was in bed, so that she could gaze through the window and think of those cosy nights she had spent in her grandmother's house. Like Pinch, she loved to listen to the sounds of faraway trains.

Peggy came to the door and announced that his tea was waiting.

"I love you, Mrs. Pinch. It's not often I mention it."

"And I love you -- Arthur."

"Shall we have tea out here? It's a lovely night. What do we have to go with it."

"Hot muffins with Miss Carstairs' kitchen garden butter. They're fresh from the stove."

"Two cats have been fighting," he reported when she returned with a terrine of steaming muffins. "I recognise the screeching of Marmaduke Reynolds."

"He must have been matched against Queen O'Scots," said Peggy. "She's the boss of all cats on her Street. She was either settling a score or enforcing discipline, I bet Marmaduke went home with a twisted face."

Pinch's praise for the kitchen garden butter was almost overwhelming. He allowed himself to slobber and collected trickles of the fat as it dribbled off his chin.

"You were talking of the King," he began. "There is a story, no more than that, about the King's drive through the village."

"I remember. It was during the war."

"1916."

"We all lined up on The Street and the King waved when we all clapped."

Pinch laughed. "That's right. Now, who was it who started the clapping instead of cheers?"

"The old man from the level crossing."

"Yes, of course. It's no more than a story but some folk say that little Sir Roland had his trousers undone when the King went through."

"Lord above! Is that why he didn't stop?"

"I don't think so. I don't think that would have bothered him. He's been a good King," he reflected. "I'm sure that his criticism after Jutland put the Navy right."

"Pinch, how could you know that?"

"I don't, for sure. It's no more than a story." He drew breath. "I could cut the man's throat. That's how I feel."

"Come indoors," said Peggy.

"There is a way. You would be in control all the time. Wistow and I would be on hand if things went wrong. Peggy, it would flush him out, I know it would. But we'd have to be quick. Tomorrow night would be our last opportunity."

She heard Gort's dog bark in the night.

"Then we'd better go ahead," she said.

There were ready to withdraw from the porch when they were distracted by some quiet movement in the lane. A white English leghorn, a hen, hesitantly trod from the grass verge and into a patch of light in the middle of the road. She had escaped her coop but only now realised how much at risk she was. She progressed slowly, often with half a step so that she paused on one foot. Her head twitched in response to any sound in the hedgerows or any hint of movement. Then she felt an immediate threat; with a flap of her wings and some extra spring in her legs she managed to scurry to the cover of Peggy's hedge-bottom. She had left behind a pool of light which changed colour as it filled with grey shadow cast by a running man

"Good grief, the front of the man." Pinch shouted, "Look, here he comes."

Sir Roland, out of breath, came striding out of the darkness. "I've been broken into," he panted. He rattled the garden gate, unable to open it cleanly.

Pinch carefully laid his smouldering pipe on the porch step.

"The church plate has gone from our safe! Pinch I'm here to report a crime! A serious crime!" He was half way up the path when the policeman in his dressing gown met him with a jabbing fist to his nose. The punch lifted the man off his feet and sent him scurrying back to the hedge bottom.

"Arthur, no!" Peggy shouted.

"My God! Look!" Sir Roland was fingering the blood from his nose and twisting his head, searching for Pinch's figure in the dark.

"That's enough, Arthur."

Pinch kicked his slippered heel into the seat of the man's trousers, pushing his face and shoulders into the dirt.

"I've come about the theft," he wept. "Nothing else."

"Run away, you bugger, and don't let Peggy or I see you until this murder's sorted."

The miscreant didn't utter another word. He crawled and stumbled off, managing to run only when he reached the Twitchels.

Pinch knocked his pipe out on the brick wall, allowed himself a last look up The Street, then followed his wife to their sitting-room. All in all, it was a night's work well done.

Chapter Eight

Another Side of a Country Yeoman

The next morning the village woke, gradually and peacefully, and with a soft voice that was familiar to all, young and old. For hundreds of years, the roads and trackways, the brook and the hillside, had welcomed each day with the same familiarity. In modern times, the sounds had learned to accommodate different houses, with a thirst for fences and hedges, and to allow different ways of doing things, but so much remained not just unchanged but also unchallenged. At eleven o'clock that morning, the Welfare Circle of village housewives would meet and arrange for Small Thin Annie to have breakfast with old Mr Withers each day; the committee would provide the wherewithal. And, a good long time before opening, the Red Lion would cluster children around the hearth of the public bar to ensure that no village infant went to school without a healthy warming up first. Pinch, knowing that a hearty breakfast would be ready for him at eight o'clock, nevertheless shared an early tuck-in - each morning, without fail - with either the gamekeeper or the poacher, sometimes one indistinguishable from the other. On market days, the village bus took people to town and brought them back again at four o'clock. Twice daily, but sometimes four times, Farmer Wistow walked his cows the length of The Street.

He had five that morning and Peggy, strolling back from the Post Office, had to walk between them before she could reach her front gate.

"Ah, Peg," said the gravel faced farmer. He had never before chanced such familiarity. "We ought to have a word, you and me. I need to tell you the truth."

Peggy had the gate open but hadn't walked through it. The cows, sensing that they were free of Wistow's immediate correction, had carried on but dispersed, so that they were in the middle and on both sides of the road.

"Not here," Peggy said with a touch of gravity. "Not while Pinch isn't here. It would be wrong for things to be said in his house without him."

She promised to meet him in less than five minutes at the fireside of The Red Lion's saloon. The place offered the right balance of seclusion and public view. So, for forty minutes the cows were left to meander up and down The Street. Folk made nothing of their presence; unattended cows were not an upset. Two made a mess on each grassy verge, while a third stood sentry; she would not be moved from the middle of the road.

Constable Pinch heard of the assignation as he delivered a court letter at the gate of Haylocks Farm. He bicycled on and was given the same news from the signalman at Cutler's Box, and again from the watermill, four miles from the village, when Mistress Brumby opened the window of the underworking and shouted the gossip at the top of her voice. The village bus, returning empty from the market town, stopped and Pinch and the driver shared a smoke; the busman did not relay the news but asked if Pinch had heard anything untoward. In each circumstance, the policeman assured the sneaks that all was in order. Farmer Wistow had alerted the husband of his need to talk with the wife.

Before Haylocks, before Cutlers and the watermill, he had met Wistow, emerging from barn doors with blood covering his forearms and much of his smock. He may have been playing midwife but Pinch didn't ask.

"Good to see you, Pinch," he said, lifting the skirt of his smock to wipe his hands. "I need to meet up with your Peggy. I don't relish the way this murder case is shaping up. Frankly, I need to step out of the shadows." They were walking across the stockyard of cracked concrete and stray ducks. A dirty coloured labrador emerged from the back of the farmhouse, looking for his master. Wistow clicked his fingers and the dog came to heel.

Pinch came straight out with it. "I don't want to intrude into the murkier side of your working life but I am going to ask you to lean on one of your contacts. The Bad Bull at Bottom Lock will be hosting a lock-in tonight. I want you to get invited, then arrange for Templar to go in your place. Half a dozen locals will be drawing a lottery. Templar's got to win."

"God, man." Wistow was weaving his hand around the dog's head; he might have been searching for foreign lumps beneath the animal's coat. "What are you up to?"

"I'm going to flush out the killer."

"Come indoors. We'll smoke in the scullery."

He called to his wife as they entered the farmhouse; a reply came from the outside: "I'm in with the geese , Horace!"

"Pinch, I'm a darned fraud," he said, cracking more eggs than he needed, some with feathers and muck stuck to their mainly white shells, into a large black frying pan. "We still like things feudal round here. People look up to me as one of the village elders. Tradesmen tip their caps when they see me and seem very pleased to do it." Smoke shimmered from a second frying pan, just as large and just as deep with dripping. "You're different. The village policeman, like the vicar and the doctor, sits apart from the general run of folk. But I'm given a respect and I don't want it. I haven't earned it and, sure as hell, there's no merit in it. I'm paid to spy on them, Pinch, and that's how it's been since the Great War."

He cut thick slices of bread, no more than six to a loaf, and laid them in the scorching beef dripping. If they tried to get out again, he prodded them with a fork.

"The picture's hardly that bleak, Wistow. You were asked to report any suspicions about a German spy in the village. That's not irregular in war-time. Damn it, man, most villagers would have said well done and get on with it. And if you carried on after the war, well, I see no difference. How many people have you told tales on? There, you've accused none."

The farmer confessed. "I had a good look at you when you first came here." He collected a pot of mustard from the kitchen window sill and carried two plates of eggs and fried bread to the table. "Tuck in, boy. I'm not having sausages until I get to the Red Lion. I wouldn't have them anywhere else."

"You were obvious about it. You tested too many tricks of the trade."

Wistow lifted his eyebrows. "I did?"

"The first time we met, you gave me two opportunities to fib to you. Once would have been suspicious. Twice was clumsy. Then you made sure that I was given chance to read a letter from your bank."

"I decided that you were honest," Wistow wiped a finger beneath his nose, adding, "By and large."

"Do you think Templar's the spy?"

"Not for the Kaiser. His sympathies lie further east, I'm afraid."

"Good lord, if it's not George Templar, and it's not you or I, you cannot suspect Edna Carstairs.

Farmer Wistow was wiping his chops with a large white napkin. "Arthur, don't rule out Mavis Reynolds. Come on, I'll show you the latest motor, I'm working on."

But Pinch stayed in his chair. "Mavis Reynolds? She moved into the village after the war was settled. It can't be her."

"I suspected Peggy's mother for a long time."

"Nonsense!"

"And when she died, Mavis Reynolds appeared for no good reason. I'm still not sure that one didn't follow the other."

"Wistow, you can't tell me that Peggy's mother was a German spy! I won't believe you!"

In the Red Lion, the children's warming-up-circle was over and there was less than an hour to go before drinking time. When Peggy walked in the back door, through the kitchen and into the saloon bar, Wistow and the landlady were sparring over the price of two plated breakfasts. The point was made that, when she had no guests upstairs, the Red Lion wanted breakfasts done with by half past eight, "So that's nine pence and you can pay now."

"How much!"

"Listen, I've got things to do. Amy will bring your sausages and eggs when they're cooked but she's too busy to tend tables. So you can pay now."

"The Queen's Head wouldn't charge above seven pence."

"Why don't you go there? The Queen's a friendly enough inn."

"She's closed."

"Well, I charge seven pence when I'm closed. When I'm open, breakfasts like you've booked are nine pence."

Wistow knew that he had secured too much of a bargain to grumble further, so he joined Peggy by the fire. They sat either side of a little round-topped table. "It's not that I've been telling lies," he began. "But perhaps you don't know the whole truth of it, so I thought we ought to talk."

"I've only ten minutes," she warned. "I've got things to do this morning and, this afternoon, I'm in the Dead Bishop's Sitter."

"Dead Bishop?"

"It's a forgotten room on the top floor of our rectory. Rather nice, actually. No, it's absolutely beautiful with old books and written accounts. I'm sure I'd uncover some maps if I looked underneath enough things."

The breakfasts arrived. Five sausages, four eggs and fried bread for the farmer. A slice of lightly poached fish, caught locally, for the policeman's wife.

"Don't tell the old lady, but they do an expert's sausage in here." He went on to explain, "The quality of a sausage is not in its flavouring, though many butchers will want to persuade you. And it's certainly not in the quality of meat; good meat should be on your Sunday lunch plate, not in your sausage. No, the secret of the sausage lies in its skin. It must be tough, so that it crisps, and keeps the fat in. You want fat sausages, who doesn't?"

"I have less than ten minutes, Mr Wistow," she reminded him.

He assured her than ten minutes was more than enough time . "My orders are not to reveal myself," he began. "But the job can't be done without my being frank with you, Mrs. Pinch." Without turning his head to look at her, he declared, "I am Farmer Wistow of the Secret Service."

Apart from an unladylike snort, which she managed to convert to a sniff at the last moment, Peggy managed to stall further reaction.

"Yes, well, it is supposed to sound incongruous. Am I the last fellow you'd suspect of spying? Then, I've got something right at least. I was recruited to keep an eye on Mistress Knightly and to spot any nefarious indications of a spy taking advantage of our quiet English setting. Neither task done, I confess with deep regret. I don't know why I am still employed."

Peggy asked discreetly, "How much do you know?"

"I know all about Miss Knightly and her letters. Of course, I don't know how much I don't know. That's part of being a secret agent, I suppose." He said, "You were told to report the progress of your investigation to George Templar. Well, my instructions are that he is likely to be arrested, tomorrow morning, for the murder of Eliza Knightly."

"Why, that's nonsense. He couldn't possibly have done it. If you're truly in the Secret Service, you must tell them to let him go."

"I wish it worked like that but, no, I'm afraid they wouldn't listen to me. But his arrest does mean that I am now Spy-catcher General 'round these parts and, ridiculous as that might sound, it's my job to make sure no further harm comes your way."

Miss Reynolds was looking through the dimpled panes of the front windows and wondering what the pair were doing inside.

"Does Pinch know what you do?"

Wistow avoided the question. "Not much gets past P.C. Pinch," he said while making the best marriage of an egg yolk and a sausage end. "Oh, please, waste no more time searching for 25 August."

"The missing letter?"

"I met Eliza the day before the murder and she passed it to me for safe keeping. You could say that it lies in the custody of the Crown. Yes, she wrote that she had surely been betrayed in the village. It seems that the Germans were trying to introduce anthrax into England by tampering with a consignment of shaving brushes. When the package was intercepted, the High Command quickly identified Knightly's lover as the source of betrayal. There was something of a to-do in the corridors of our War Office at the time. The whole story of the shaving brushes would have been kept quiet but the damned affair got reported in the papers."

"What about the censor? It seems to me that nothing would have been printed without the War Office being in on it, which suggests ..."

"Yes?"

Peggy was still thinking it through. "Either, the cat was already out of the bag or our Secret Service intended the leak as part of a further scheme. What did Miss Knightly say about it?"

"She gave no details. I think that she was too frightened to look for any clues."

"And what about you? Do you have any suspicions?"

"Oh, I suppose 'feelings' rather than 'suspicions'. It is better that we follow any trail of evidence. The War Office is confident that you will come up with something."

When they were standing in the middle of The Street, Wistow with his cows, Mrs. Pinch with her letters for the Post Office, she asked, "Do you get paid?"

"A simple acknowledgement at Christmas. I used to enjoy being part of the game. Oh, I am a one case wonder, if wonder is the right word, but the War Office sends me all sorts of tit-bits of information. Quite, quite fascinating. Do you know, I am responsible for reporting the condition of all railway bridges in the area? They suppose that being a farmer is the perfect disguise for a job like that. Well, just look at that, Mrs. Pinch. We haven't seen ducks near our ford for three years. They were all over my yard this morning and now - what a delight! I shall include the observation in my report of our conversation."

He made some farm-like noises to bring the cows to order, then continued to drive them to the top of The Street. The place was messier for their being there and some grass verges had been gnawed unevenly but no gardens had been touched and, even if Dolly Johnson might one day wonder what had happened to the discarded straw hat she was saving for Guy Fawkes, the village was no worse for the cows having been left alone.

Peggy stopped in the middle of the road. The vicar was striding towards them, waving a hand in the air and calling, "A good morning! Mrs. Pinch! I say!"

Peggy walked a couple of steps towards the hurrying vicar. For a moment, she doubted that he would stop in time but his long legs seemed to be equipped with extraordinary brakes.

"I'm worried." He pulled at the black curl of his goatie beard. "Very worried and rather desperate. It's the Harvest Festival. I've published that we'll be holding it on St Luke's Day but, Goodness, that's but three weeks away. I had so wanted the church to be overflown with decorations. This being my first year, you see. I've pictured it with sheaves of corn, fruit and vegetables, and flowers of course. But now I realise that such a display won't just happen, with no one to light the spark, and I've not the say-so to make it happen. Too new, you see. It's such a curse, being fresh to the parish. I need someone to take the lead, to encourage others to bring forth the produce."

"Like your maid," said Peg.

"And yourself, Mrs. Pinch. Everyone tells me that you run all constabulary affairs in our little nook."

"I was talking about Polly, your help."

"Oh yes, she's a real help but, again, so new."

"I know that she longs to be of service."

"You've noticed? I must say that I've rather overlooked her."

"She's in love."

"Polly? In love? Polly in love? Oh, I don't think so. She knows no more about romance and kissing and what-not, than I do." He added in haste, "Which is nothing."

"Then, spare just a few seconds to look."

"Mind, I must say that the lucky fellow should turn up sharpish; she's too much of a catch to miss."

Peggy sighed. "The Harvest Festival will go just fine, vicar." With the vicar's acquiescence, she turned away from match-making and thought more seriously about the remnant of stair carpet.

"You do the paperwork?" he continued, not wanting her to walk off. "Yes, it is much the same in businesses managed from home. There is much evidence Shakespeare's mother kept accounts for her husband."

"Shakespeare's mother?" As if it had never occurred to her that someone so famous would have a mother.

"His father was a glove maker."

"Of course! And I leave to my wife my second best glove. I knew that I heard it somewhere."

The vicar laughed out loud. "Oh, very good! Oh, dear me, second best glove!" He spluttered as he tried to absorb his mirth. "My, well I must make it the last line of my sermon." He walked up The Street, shaking his head.

Peggy stood in the middle of the lane, unable to share the joke. But she would get her own back. 'Every dog has her day,' she said in her head. "Perhaps I shall laugh in church."

"Oh, I shouldn't do that, dear," said Edna Carstairs as she arrived, unnoticed, at Peggy's shoulder. She lead her friend towards the floral border of her front verge. "It must be two weeks since we shared morning tea and scones." Then: "I am afraid that we shall need to involve the Rural Dean. It's not to be done lightly, so early in an incumbency, but the matter will not resolve itself."

"The matter?"

"The beard. The new vicar's beard. Well, we can't be having it, Peggy. There have been secret meetings about it. Meetings after midnight in Mavis Reynold's back bedroom. Mind, Edna Carstairs would have nothing to do with that. As well you know. But the issue remains and remain it cannot."

"It is such a small beard," Peggy argued, stooping to pick up a cluster of pebbles which had fallen into the bed. "And I think that he's brought something particular to the Rectory. Flowerbeds around the front borders. That never used to be.

And kittens are scampering over the back paddock. Tell me, how many years it is since you saw that."

"This has nothing to do with it!" declared the old schoolteacher. "Mavis Reynolds, just last night -she came in for cribbage, only the two of us - and I told her that the vicar may well have returned several of the rooms back to their old character, but it has nothing to do with the discomfort of having a vicar with a beard in his pulpit."

"Are you sure it's the rooms that are nothing to do with it and not the beard."

Edna resorted to snapping. "Quite sure and I do like to keep those stones on the soil for air," she explained. "And, what's more, I think it's the maid not the vicar who has taken care of the rooms. She never comes out of the place."

"Hardly a beard at all," Peggy persisted, and dropped the stones into the soil. "I think we should wait until matters have taken their course,"

"Don't talk gobble-de-goop, girl. What do you mean?" Edna Carstairs lowered her voice, "Something's afoot, Peggy. Mavis was round my scullery door before seven o'clock this morning. She saw you and the vicar in the Twitchels last night, beneath the trees. She says you met him there with his motorcycle. Like some dopey adolescent girl!"

Peggy tried to stall herself from thinking aloud. "You're right, Edna, something is up with our Reverend Sullivan. Yes, we met by accident in the middle of the night and this morning he talks as if it didn't happen. He was in a similar muddle last night. Edna, I don't think he remembers things. I think that whole episodes don't lodge in his mind."

"Good Lord, you're serious."

Peggy sighed and listened to some second thoughts before she replied, "I'm afraid, I am deadly serious. Please, say nothing."

"Of course," her old friend assured her. Then: "Perhaps a word with Doctor Meriweather?"

The clock chimed the three-quarter hour. "I'm supposed to be with the Dead Bishop." Peggy stepped backwards and turned to face uphill. "And as for this murder? I don't think the matter will be properly solved until the new vicar and his maid are betrothed."

"Oh, my goodness. Yes, well. I do seem to have missed more than I'm used to."

Peggy tried to express her own doubts. "Edna, I've missed something. Something I said that was crucial, but I let it slip by without noticing it. Something very obvious. But, blast it all, I can't get at it."

Chapter Nine

Violence

When Peggy Pinch ran a fingertip along the shelves of books, in the Dead Bishop's Sittingroom, she wasn't reading the spines but savouring the textures of leathers and hides in the different bindings.

There were seven journals, with backs frayed and clumsily repaired, handwritten by consecutive vicars before 1920. When Peggy removed them, an old letter spilled forward from its hiding place in the bookcase. Unaddressed and unsigned, it was a letter from a previous woman of the house for the benefit of vicarage wives in years to come. It was sincere and charming and reflected that sense of an incumbent being no more than a guardian until someone else took over. Peggy leafed through the delicately written notes, looking for any reference to the war. But she found only domestic discussion. She sensed a dispute when the wife argued that the long-case clock should always be placed in the front parlour, so that visitors would be aware that they were taking the vicar's valuable time. But, nowadays, Grandfather stood in the lobby, at the foot of the stairs. Peggy imagined one of Sullivan's predecessors explaining that his parishioners should feel no time pressure, but callers may be reminded of their punctuality, or otherwise, when they were welcomed through the front door. How close was Peggy's musing to the truth? Peggy returned the letter to its cubby-hole behind the collection of chalk drawings of the parish treasures, including the missing church plate. Here, someone had noted: 'Not seen since bloody murder in T.S. and H.'

There were three different county histories, two sets of war commentaries and, a small volume published by the vestry, being a brief monograph on the Pleasures of Small Gardens by one Arthur Pinch. Peggy had heard nothing of this book; she opened the Sitter window and perched herself on the broad oak ledge.

It was a lovely morning. The sunshine had found new colours in the fruit garden below and sounds of a beagle chase came in from the fields. The vicar and his maid were practising croquet on the lawn and, thank goodness, their voices had those qualities of a man and woman who think that no one else can hear them. A black locomotive had broken down on the valley line and heavy plant passed through the village on their way to repair. The incongruous noise was more than compensated by excited interest along The Street. Peggy spent twenty minutes in this open air, with Pinch's book between her hands, before telling herself off for getting distracted.

She sat at the mahogany topped table and assembled her sources of evidence. The old clerical journals. From the police house, she had brought the wartime Occurrence Books, thick and heavily bound volumes whose quality made the modern issues look like casual note pads. And the letters of Eliza Knightly, lifelong spinster of this parish. Peggy got to work. She trawled through Spinster Knightly's letters, noting any occasions when the German soldier seemed to suspect that his authorities were on to him. It was boring and unrewarding work. After three quarters of an hour, Peggy had identified only five dates worthy of further investigation.

Then she went to the vicarage journal for 25 August 1916. There, pasted in like a memento in a scrapbook, was a newspaper cutting about the interception of shaving brushes. A note in fountain ink annotated the clipping as the Daily Mirror for that Friday morning. A further note in the margin, written on the slant, recorded "Much bitterness in our parish as Eliza Knightly, spinster, is thought to have passed crucial information to a young man, irregular in these parts and evidently not fighting for his country, in an ill-fitting brown suit. This writer is at a loss to suggest any secrets lodged in our little backwater!"

Her mind strayed from her studies. Still, she was bothered by the vicar's laughter at her expense. She needed to settle the score, somehow - but settled in a way that satisfied without causing the vicar's discomfort. She decided to write a cheeky nursery rhyme and hide it in the bookshelves.

She pulled some notepaper towards her, picked up a pencil and chewed the end. Just like she had been told off for as a young girl. She was determined to make it the rudest nursery rhyme ever. No-one would find it for years and no-one, but a smug Peggy Pinch, would know who had written it.

She began: "Our vicar has a goatie beard." Then, immediately, went to lines three and four: "And everywhere the vicar went, The goaties had to go." But what about the second line? "Our vicar has a goatie beard …. Ah yes! Yes, yes!" She scribbled the missing line on the notepad, folded the page into quarters and tucked it behind a random page in the vicar's journal. She was chuckling, "That'll learn him," as Polly came in at half past one with a pot of tea and a side plate of open cucumber sandwiches. "There's nothing to worry about," she promised. "Sullivan's gone off on his visits and won't be back. No one knows that you are here." She noticed the letters. "I won't ask what you're up to. It seems very private and it's better it stays that way."

"Has he said anything to you?" Peggy inquired.

"Anything? Oh no, Mr Sullivan doesn't say things."

Left alone and idling, Peggy returned to the vicars' journals, leafing through each until she found the entries, close to the dates she had noted from Eliza Knightly's letters. It seemed to be another fruitless diversion at first. She went through the same procedure with the Police logs and, five times out of five, the evidence coincided.

She stood up, turned away from the desk and looked through the window, across the vicarage lawn into the valley. "Good Lord, it's true. Lord, we do have a German spy in our village."

Then the door flew open and Sir Roland was there, his lips drawn back from his bare teeth and his eyes on fire.

"What are you doing!"

He went straight for her shoulders, squeezing them so hard that she was sure he wanted to pull them apart. He hauled her off her feet and threw her against a corner bookcase. At once, his hands were at her skirt, forcing it upwards. She kicked, but it meant nothing. She tossed her head from side to side which provoked him to seize her mouth between his thumb and forefinger. But he had no yen to kiss her. He turned her. He pushed her backwards onto the table top. Peggy was fighting. She felt all her strength go to her arms and legs but they were flailing, hitting nothing and tiring her out.

He forced her dress above her hips, his long fingers tearing anything that was in their way. He held her knees high in the air then pressed down on them until her thighs felt ready to be ripped from their sockets.

"No!" she shouted. "I'll not let you!"

Poke his eyes, she kept telling herself but she was throwing her head from side to side and was unable to see them. Christ! He'd managed to pull his trousers and underpants down! She screamed. She screamed again and kept it going. Then, thank God, a crash of pottery sent him backwards. He dropped to the floor, blood already spewing from the back of his skull.

Polly was standing there with two hands over her mouth and her eyes ready to pop from her forehead. "My God! God, help me! I've murdered him!"

Peggy rolled over, spewing phlegm from her nose and throat. She coughed as she dropped to the floor, gripping her stomach. "No, you haven't, Polly. You mustn't let yourself think that. Listen." She took the little woman in her arms, shaking her shoulders and putting her own face up against hers. "You mustn't tell anybody what he was trying to do. I couldn't bare it. The questions and the looks and …"

"Of course, I won't tell," said the maid. "I - I have never killed anyone before."

"He attacked me because he wanted to know what I was doing. I screamed and you came in."

"And murdered him."

"No, you cracked a pot over his head. That's all."

"I hate men," the maid said simply. "Don't you, Peggy?"

"Only those I have met." She felt herself wanting to ramble on about anything. "Now, we must leave everything as it is, while I call Arthur. He knows how to get out of messes like this."

Peggy guided the woman down the staircase and told her to stay in the kitchen, no matter what. Then she used the phone in the vicarage hallway and called Little Home Farm and a private number for the Signal Box before finding Pinch in the Bad Bull at Bottom Lock.

"Come to the vicarage at once. I've got another body."

He told her that, even if he got red-faced and panting, he was still a twenty minute bike ride away. "Stay away from the corpse," he said.

She sat at the bottom of the staircase and tried to keep her arms close to her body. She felt very cold. She started to shiver and let her nose run as her head was counting the beat of her knees trying to knock together. One-two-three-four. One-two-three-four. She wanted to curl up. Her muscles on her left side started to spasm, contract, and pull her leg and arm up to her chest. Counting in her head was her best way of keeping her senses, she said.

The door bell rang after seven minutes, not twenty, and Peggy thanked heaven that he had managed to get a lift. But when she opened the front door, she found Mistress Nevers, standing like a fallen woman on the steps of the workhouse.

"I'm sorry. Reverend Sullivan is not here, Miss Nevers."

"He won't be. He's having tea in Laurel Cottage. You're the only one I can tell, Peggy. I have no-one else."

"Miss Nevers, things are going on and … look, you better come in. We'll tuck ourselves away in the vicar's front parlour for a few moments."

"I've not been in here before," she said, looking around. "Will you be doing regular teas from now on, Mrs. Pinch? Holding tea and sandwiches for housewives in the village? Many of us have said how proper it would be, the vicar having no vicar's wife. I'll take the seat away from the window."

"What do you want to tell me, Miss Nevers."

She nodded. "You know. You know," she nodded again, "Don't you?"

Polly Adam, quickly in tune with what was happening, stepped into the room with a pot of tea for two and open cucumber sandwiches. "Constable Pinch has arrived." She gave Miss Nevers a faraway pretended knowing smile. "I've put him in the scullery with the cats."

"Thank you, Polly," said Peggy, adopting a slightly rough edge to her voice that went with auditioning for her new role. "Now, then, Maud …"

"I'm having a baby."

Peggy found herself saying, "I hope you're able to see what a blessing that is."

Miss Nevers, suddenly aware of sensitivities which had not before occurred to her, chewed on a lip, then dipped her head. There was a brave touch to her voice. She was far from tears, but her tummy was tense and her breathing was shallow. Drawing in deep would have made her chest hurt, she knew. "There are so many different factors to think about. I'm all-but beside myself, Peggy."

"You mustn't think that you're on your own. We can seem a grouchy gaggle of old hens when we are on The Street and the weather's against us, but we're always here for one another. It's a long time since I've tasted quite such nice salad sandwiches." Peggy said carefully, "I've heard that Bill Wheeler is on his own?"

Maud Nevers tried a little smile. "That's the difference between a policeman's wife and a vicar's wife," she said without any rebuke. "The lady of the rectory would never have asked."

The touch of humour felt like progress. As Peggy sat forward to play mother, Miss Nevers said plainly, "William has said nothing to me. That's what makes it so awkward."

"I can't think of a fellow more likely to step up to his responsibilities," Peggy remarked. "You haven't told him?"

The woman hesitated, "I don't know if it is that simple."

Peggy heard Pinch's heavy footsteps in the room above. She comforted herself with an infantile certainty that now that he had been told about the problem, he would sort it out. If Peggy kept quiet and pretended to have had nothing to do with all the things that had gone wrong, Pinch would make them go away.

"I never thought that Mavis Reynolds would start the tittle-tattle. You know that we've been friends for years. She doesn't even know! I have told no-one! Yet she goes whispering to Mistress Knightly. I shall never forgive her!"

"Yes, you will," Peggy softly said. "Plenty of that goes on in this house. In fact, I fancy that a blessing on forgiveness was one of the reasons you rang the front door bell." She smiled, "Sometimes we need a way of giving ourselves permission, don't we?"

"Peggy, will you tell Willie for me?"

"Willie? Oh, you mean Bill. No, Maud, don't deny yourselves such a lovely moment."

For the time, Maud Nevers went red in the face.

"Won't you find out for me? What does he want to do?" Tears were welling in her eyes now. "I've got to know how he reacts."

"You mean, is Wheeler willing? I shall take some soundings, Maud, but no more than that. I've learned to do no matchmaking."

When the time came, Mistress Nevers asked to leave through the Ladies Parlour and across the terrace behind the house. She said that she was going to wander down the Waddie and cut through the side path of one of the cottages.

At five and twenty to five, Arthur Pinch carried a loaded tea-tray from the vicarage kitchen to the front parlour.

His wife was five paces behind him, balancing more than enough cake on two mock silver stands. "But Pinch, he was a dead body. I prodded him. For God's sake, I know a proper corpse when I finger one."

"If that's the case, he came alive again and escaped through the Dead Bishop's window. Dead men don't get up and walk, Peggy; I've searched the house and the three of us are alone. I've put the maid to bed."

"Arthur?"

"Oh, don't come that with me. Putting a pretty maiden to bed with delicacy is one of the first skills a copper learns. She's in the vicar's bedroom, directly above us. I couldn't risk her being alone at the top of the house and at the back. I've never made sense of this building. It's all over the place." He added, "This room's for receiving visitors, not for living in," comparing it to the police house parlour.

"There's a Ladies Parlour which overlooks the back lawn," Peggy remarked. "I think vicars spend most of their hours in their study."

"Yes, writing sermons."

"Or talks for the Church of England Men's Society."

"Where's Reverend Sullivan?"

"In his potting shed. I've told him what's happened but he didn't seem to take it in. He carried on as if I hadn't spoken to him. Peggy, our rector's a poorly man."

They sat quietly, conscious of the uneven ticking of the mantelpiece clock and the spitting of fresh logs in the grate. "Eat up, Arthur. Cakes and puddings are the two best blessings of visiting our vicarage. Edna will be here at five with replenishments and she won't want to see any left overs from the first course."

"I'm uneasy about leaving Edna Carstairs and poor Polly alone this evening," Pinch sighed.

"Then you must sit with them. I've said so all along. Oh, really, Pinch. You know that I will be perfectly safe in the Bad Bull. Both the vicar and Templar will keep an eye on me, and our parish spy-catcher will be hiding upstairs. Your best place is here." Peggy tapped the arm of her chair. "First, I need your help, Pinch. I want you to stand on the terrace and see if you can hear anything spoken at the foot of the staircase."

"Something is bothering you."

"Something that won't go away. Wistow says that it's not important."

Pinch took his empty pipe from hia pocket. "Everything is important if it doesn't make sense."

He left the front room, walked through the Ladies Parlour, leaving the intervening door open, and watched from beyond the French window. Peggy stood at the telephone and recited her naughty rhyme about the vicar's goatie beard.

"I can see you plain enough," he reported. "But no-one could have heard you from that distance."

"So. There's no other explanation. Someone else was in this house when I thought I was alone with the maid." She went back to her armchair. "Fiddlesticks, Pinch. It's all fiddlesticks and I want to know who?"

Before five o'clock, Pinch's security measures were in place. Jacoby and two assistants were patrolling the grounds, two with shotguns and the third with a sling shot. Pinch was uneasy about that third lad. A sling shot is no more deadly than a shotgun but country folk would not accept it in the same way. Goodness, it would sound dreadful if things came to an inquest. But he trusted Jacoby's judgement and gave no voice to his concern.

Edna Carstairs arrived and suggested an evening at cards. "You've had more than enough to eat today, Arthur Pinch." She checked on the sleeping Polly Adam, lighting a small fire in the bedroom grate and shaking the drapes before settling down

The sparrow-hawk perched on the parapet, high above everything, her yellow eyes as large and hard as a child's toy marbles. She twitched. She spied. Yet, she let no one know what she was up to.

Chapter Ten

Dolly in Jodhpurs

At five, Dolly Johnson was seated on a three-legged stool on the narrow terrace of her garden, waiting for Mavis Reynolds. She had been given less than two hours to get ready for her birthday party but she didn't need to think twice about her rig. The rail of party dresses was ignored and she had no wish to curl her hair. Fashionable shoes, stockings and ribboned blouses were out of the question. She went straight to the spare room and took the jodhpurs from her back wardrobe; she had bought these at the Church bazaar two years ago, knowing that anything donated by the best dressed lady in Back Lane would be of lasting quality. The softened leather of the inside legs kept her snug. The leather patch encasing her seat was, she decided, eminently smackable.

"Short like a boy's," she instructed when she heard Miss Reynold's approach from behind.

"But Dolly, your lovely hair!"

"Short back and sides and thin on top. Be quick, Mavis. I must be ready before a quarter to six."

So, clip by clip, ringlets of Dolly's Johnson's blonde hair fell to the crazy paving and, when nothing was left but stubble, out came the cut-throat razor to finish the job. "Have you taken enough off the top?" asked Dolly

"Which side do want the parting?"

"Will it go on the left?"

"It will go where it is told," Miss Reynold's replied. She felt that she had been tricked into taking advantage of a simpleton, but rarely had she seen Dolly so determined.

But for the bath towel over her shoulders, Dolly Johnson would have been bare-breasted throughout the encounter on her back terrace. When the hair-dressing was finished off with a finger of lard well rubbed in, she conceded, "I'm hopeless with a bodice. Mavis, you're going to have to squeeze me in." She asked her neighbour to collect the garment laid out on her bed. Once again, she was impressed by the quality of clothes which Dolly had acquired. "I got it at the school-jumble, last Christmas. It does a really good push up. You'll see what is does to them."

The finishing touch, a leather flying helmet, certainly impressed the motorcyclist.

"You are finely dressed," said Reverend Sullivan when he led her to the waiting machine. "Imagine that we are but one figure. Hold yourself against my back and lean when I lean."

She did just as she had been told. Once settled on the pillion saddle, she pushed herself into his back, wrapping her arms around his waist and tucking her head between his shoulders. "Are you going to drive me fast?" she asked as he splashed through the ford and accelerated up the hill. He shouted something. She couldn't make out the words but she held on, her clasped hands creeping up to his chest until she could sense the strength of his muscles. She wondered if, inch by inch, her fingers might find their way through the zip of his jacket and the buttons of his shirt. Then she closed her eyes and resolved to waste no more time thinking but to savour every exhilarating moment of the ride.

The Bad Bull at Bottom Lock was the local pub for surrounding farms and an isolated community of railway and water company cottages. A nearby private school provided good business when parents visited or masters came and went. It wasn't surprising that when word got round that Dolly Johnson's birthday party was likely to be peculiar, the place was filled with regulars while people from Peggy's village saw that their business was to stay away.

The landlord had set aside an alcove of two pews and a heavy bench, lacquered black, with vicious screw-heads proud of the timber joints. The large table between the pews had been changed for a lighter one.

"Look at all those books," remarked the vicar, gesturing to the shelf above the portrait of Wellington. "Not one of them's to be read. Like sorry spinsters in a row, they are."

"Or, like sorry spinsters, they will each be taken home by stealth before the month's end," joked Peggy.

"What are we doing here!" Dolly screeched. "We don't even like each other!"

"It's your birthday, Dolly!" Peggy exclaimed.

"Months ago, that was. I only came because I've never ridden on the back of a motorcycle and when Constable Pinch said 'Who's for a whizz through the lanes in the dark?' I said, 'Me first.' "

"And a delightful pillion, you were, dear."

Dolly hadn't settled in her pew before she produced a handful of cigarette cards from the lining of the flying helmet and spread them on the table. "Oh don't 'dear' me for pity's sake! You've hardly said more than Good Day to me, the whole time you've been there!"

Templar chipped in, "You've certainly dressed for the part!"

"Oi, Big Nose, who are you?"

That stopped the exchanges.

The publican's daughter with a paper hat on her head delivered the birthday cake, flickering with candles. She had hurriedly placed clumsy figures of pink icing to spell Dolly in the middle.

Templar pampered his swollen nose with a tartan handkercheif. "You are right to ask, Miss Johnson," he conceded. "Horace Wistow was supposed to be here but had to withdraw at the last moment. I am his replacement."

"But I don't even know you," protested Dolly. "This is a stupid arrangement." Without further introduction, she addressed the ciagarettes cards on the table. "Who's got what? That's what we're here for, isn't it?"

Everyone leaned forward as their eyes scanned the selection but only modest trading went on. The participants, suitably diverted, agreed that the tobacco makers had flooded the market with Numbers Eight and Seventeen, and that the picture of the Winter Grand Prix was often bleary round the edges. No-one had seen a copy of Number Twenty One.

Then the solicitor announced: "I expect to be arrested in the morning. They'll charge me with that old lady's murder and, once they list the murderers in my family, they'll consign me to follow them. I shall be hung within a month, although I promise each of you, I had nothing to do with it."

The Reverend Sullivan was just as nervous. He had selected two black whiskers beneath his ear and seemed determined to tug them out. "If they arrest you, Templar, they will throw me in prison as well. I say, I've done little that is wrong. Maybe, I am guilty of misjudgement. That's what my blessedly rotund and rumbustious Rural Dean has decreed. But that is all. I shall be identified as one of a pair and condemned for singular naivety"

"Then why should they arrest you?" ask Peggy.

"No!" shouted Dolly, drawing startled looks from the crowd in the other arm of the bar. "Don't say anything more! Oh God." She buried her face in her hands

"Evidence, my young woman," he said with despair rather than flamboyance. "Evidence, circumstantial but compelling." He sighed, "And Sunday was to be my best of all days. The Harvest Sunday falls on the feast of St Luke and I have my best ever sermon prepared. Perhaps I should lodge it in the Dead Bishop's Sittingroom. Is that what you think, Peggy Pinch? Should it be labelled, prepared but undelivered?"

"What nonsense," Peggy declared. "All this talk has nothing to do with the murder of Eliza Knightly. What was your fault, Reverend?"

But he mistook the question. "My fault is a lack of sensitivity to the spiritual needs of the non-believer. I am that clergyman, famous for advising a couple to baptise their infant in a ditch. They came to church for no other reason and I told them natural water would be sufficient for them. That's why I lost my previous living and was cast out to the wilderness of your little village."

"Blow on the candles, Dolly."

"It's not even my birthday! Not for six months, it's not. Don't you see what she's done? She's persuaded you both to come here and say how guilty you are, when she knows all along how Eliza Knightly died." Without warning, Dolly Johnson gave way to a torrent of tears. "Oh, you can't understand. None of you can understand what I've done." She tried to stem the flow with the backs of her hands. "You're both so brave, facing up to what people think of you, knowing that they are going to hang you. But I'm too frightened to speak up. I can't take it!"

Reverend Sullivan intervened. "I promised Pinch that I would have Dolly home before nine o'clock. He has placed a prohibition on my riding a motorcycle around the village after bedtime."

Peggy was already wrapping a slice of birthday cake in tissue paper. "Dolly, do you want to take portions for Cart and Gort?"

"Cart and Gort? Why ever should I?"

"What about Maud and Mavis? Mavis, for doing your hair."

She said, with little enthusiasm, "You'll have to bring them. I've nowhere to put them on the back of the motorbike."

Dolly's change of mood made her costume appear ridiculous rather than bazaar, drawing some disparagement as Sullivan led her through the bar-room and into the car park.

Their departure brought a few minutes quiet to the party table. Templar tried to sooth his swelling nose while Peggy was determined that she would not be the first to speak. She saw that the barmaid was wanting to approach them, but Peggy shook her head.

"I am accused by Deborah Twinn. Her years with T.S. and H have been well spent. She has assembled a believable case, although not enough to merit immediate arrest. It won't take them long to collect some corroboration."

They both sensed some increased interest from customers in the pubic bar. The word was out that some ticklish fun might be expected now that Peggy and Templar were alone. Peggy, aware of their secret escapade and not without a liking for fun, waited for someone to make a first move.

Now, the awkward solicitor spoke with shivering lips, giving a flubbery texture to his voice. He began, "I promised …"

Peggy interrupted smartly, "Pardon?"

"I said I promised …"

"Yes? You promised? Promised to do what? Speak up, I can hardly hear you."

He cleared his throat. "I promised to do you a disservice if ever I got the chance. My coming here wasn't quite as I pretended. That's to say, it wasn't the whole truth. Wistow was supposed to be taking part in a game of 'dare' this evening but withdrew and put me in his place. With four of the old codgers of this place, I drew lots. The winner's place was to accept a commission to pinch a named bottom."

"I'm sorry. I didn't catch you. Permission to steal something."

"No, no. Pinch."

"Yes, Mrs. Pinch. That's me. What are you going to steal? Now are you going to speak loudly or clearly or is this going to carry on all night?"

"Five of us drew lots before you got here." He was speaking loud enough for all to hear. "The winner's place was to accept a commission to pinch a named bottom."

"Let me guess which name."

"I cannot say that it wouldn't give me a couple of seconds pleasure, but, don't worry, as soon as the game was explained to me, I decided that I would fail the challenge. "

"Oh but you must play the part to the full, Mr Templar. It's a question of responsibility. Surely, it's not your place to spoil a well worn tradition. Anything less would disappoint my opinion of you. Of course, I promise to make it as impossible as I can. You wouldn't expect an easy ride, would you? " She placed an empty glass on the table top. "I'll have a Worthington White, please."

She added vacantly, "Who said someone is willing?"

"Someone is willing? I have no idea."

"I am sure it was in *David Copperfield*." She glanced at the row of books above them, but she couldn't read the spines in the dim light.

"I think that Dolly Johnson is a deserving case. I think we should protect her from the consequences of her silliness."

"I can't believe that she's done anything serious," Peggy replied. "Certainly no murder."

"Shortly before the death, she made a blatant attempt to alter Miss Knightly's will."

"Dolly Johnson? I can't believe that. She wouldn't know how to. I doubt she can write an intelligible Christmas card."

Templar explained. "She was called in to witness the original document and noticed the open bureau where Miss Knightly kept her papers. She returned, later in the evening and was caught at the desk, crossing out names and printing her own. A messy attempt, Mrs. Pinch, messy and heavy handed. The old lady chased her into the back garden. She had her up against a fence and was sticking the business of a hoeing fork from Dolly's top to toe."

"Dolly was screaming at the top of her voice, no doubt," said Peggy as she sniffed over the top of her ale.

"She was shouting that Eliza had passed information to a German spy."

"An old story," Peggy remarked, recalling the marginalia in the vicar's journal. "Dolly got it all wrong, of course. I think they were seen by Little Thin Annie and Polly Adam. I can't be sure, but the pair were overheard debating what to do. Miss Reynolds saw them and she mentioned it to Edna Carstairs who used to be our schoolteacher and she told me." She sipped her beer and pursed her lips. "I asked for White. This is a Bass."

Templar was sure that he had asked for Worthington White and had even taken a taste before returning to their table. "No, no. I'll nip to the bar and change it."

"Don't make a fuss. Simply order another.".

Left alone, Peggy again wondered if a copy of *David Copperfield* might be on the top shelf. She could not reach them without help, so she climbed on the supporting rung between the legs of her chair. She gripped the shelf and raised her face so that she could read the titles. She lifted one foot from the support and bent her knees, giving herself the freedom to push her bottom out, no more than the required inch of two. Now or never, he would take his best opportunity. When she heard him walking back to the table, the tip of her tongue pressed against her front teeth in preparation for his naughty thumb and forefinger. She closed her eyes, she held for breath and wished that common talk would start again in the pub.

Chapter Eleven

A Maid in the First Best Bed

Blood orange dawn fractured the canopy of trees in the vicarage orchard and two streams of pipe-smoke, one with a more fruity hue than the other, curled their ways skywards from the log pile behind the grass cutters shed. When a railway whistle reached up from the valley floor, one pipe-smoker reached for a large night-walkers watch from the pocket of his corduroy trousers while the other fished a more decorative example from his waistcoat. Together, they listened intently, then nodded when they heard the clatter of the signal arm and, only in their imaginations, the changing of the points. Jacoby's two assistants had been sent home. He and Pinch shared a sense of a night shift having been done.

Edna Carstairs had played baby sitter until two in the morning, freeing up Pinch for the fourth man in the grounds. When Peggy arrived home, Edna marched from the top to the bottom of the village and prepared a bed for herself in the police house parlour, so that Peggy would not be alone at home. Then, at six o'clock and at her own suggestion, she returned to the vicarage where she prepared breakfast for all involved and undertook to wait on Polly Adam until all trace of fear had expired.

When Reverend Sullivan stepped into his bedroom, Polly was sitting up and eating breakfast from a tray on her lap. Miss Carstairs had made sure that she was well covered with a dressing gown and shawl, and a headscarf at her side in case she needed to lie down. She looked especially little now that she was in the broad double bed which the Diocese afforded for its vicarage. She had brought her long dark hair forward over one shoulder and she still gave the impression of looking up from a bottom corner. But, on the whole and thanks to the retired schoolma'am, she was well presented.

"I see you found the rough copy of my sermon for Sunday," he said.

Five pages from a fountain pen lay on the eiderdown. "I'm sorry but I have suggested a few alterations. I hope you don't mind."

"Oh, not at all," he said, immediately interested in her contribution. "I had no idea you were a Bible reader."

"You see, that's where you've misstepped, Mr Sullivan."

"No, you can't go on calling me Mr Sullivan."

"Vicar?"

" 'Rev', when we are alone. I've always wanted to be called Rev. Most clerics run away from it but I've always thought it quite - " He shrugged his shoulders and chuckled. "-Trendy."

She couldn't grasp the trendiness but conceded with a smiled, "Yes. 'Rev' it is."

He sat on the bottom corner of the bed. "Now, my misstep?"

"Your congregation here are mostly Bible readers. They talk of reading a page a day. So, you've got to take them further. Yes, mention Luke because he is your text but then, move on. Southwell on Joyfulness, I thought."

"My word," he whispered.

The girl explained. "I've only ever had one boyfriend. He was a curate and not doing well, so we studied a lot together." She added, "He discarded me for someone more proper," as if she could expect nothing better from a man.

Edna Carstairs arrived to retrieve the breakfast tray. "I think you have been in here long enough, vicar," she said, very schoolma'amish, disturbed by his sitting on the young woman's bed.

"Yes," he conceded hesitantly. "I'll take these papers and study your amendments very carefully."

Before he reached the door, she asked, "How was Dolly, last night?"

"Dolly?" he said. He was half in and half out of the room and wanting to shield behind the door. "Oh, you know. Top form. Yes, she was on top form." But he immediately returned to the bedroom. "Constable Pinch searched the house last night and noticed that it is possible to view both the front and back gardens of Wayback Cottage from the passage window, outside your room. Did you see anything that might count? Anything that might help, Polly?"

She shook her head. "I don't spend my time standing in passageways, spying on your neighbours."

Chapter Twelve
The Special Detective Officer

Miss Deborah Twinn made her statement at 7.45 a.m. in the market town's police station. Two detectives were borrowed from a neighbouring force; their experience showed. The statement filled less than three quarters of a page and was supplemented by unrecorded questions and answers. The interview was conducted by the older and fatter detective, whom the junior called Ray although not in the company of others. He draped his suit jacket over the back of a chair and stayed on his feet. He wore braces on his trousers and an ugly bulbous ring on each of his middle fingers. They looked like the rings that poulterers attached to the legs of condemned fowls. The second detective said nothing but slouched against the ledge of a barred window. The clock on the wall had stopped. The witness answered all of the questions with colourful detail. This was unusual and offered a story which did not add up. After forty-five minutes, Miss Twinn was allowed to go home and the policemen smoked in the station yard.

"She'd have danced seven bleeding veils if we had asked her," fat Ray said as he squeezed a fag end from his mouth.

In the front office, Desk Sergeant Hawk's rosy cheeks ballooned, fit to burst.

"Look lively! The Dep!"

Slamming the Property Register shut, he turned to the boy clerk. "Turf those sods out of the tea room. And see the parade room's tidy."

He told the constable at the typewriter to make himself scarce and was pushing the station cat from the mantelpiece when the Deputy Chief Officer of the police area swung through the double doors.

"We have a Bible in the station?"

"Aye aye, sir!"

"Let's have it to hand. Let's have it to hand," he repeated as he strode through the enquiry office and got to the bottom of the stairs before he asked for the inspector.

"Aye aye, sir. Good morning, sir. I've got to say how good it is to see you."

"No, you haven't got to say anything, Sergeant Hawk. My motorcycle's out front. Get it taken care of."

"Consider it done, Dep." Hawk called up the staircase, "The inspector is not on duty today, actually."

"Oh, he's on duty. I promise you, he's on duty. Get 'im in!"

"Aye aye, sir!"

"Where are they?"

But the sergeant had scurried off. The Deputy Chief stood still on the landing, cocked an eye and nodded when he heard people talking in the inspector's office. The thickly painted oak door drifted open to his touch.

" 'Struth, a civilian."

Fat and hairy and so broad necked that he could not do his top button up, Farmer Horace Wistow was seated at the inspector's desk, bringing a telephone conversation to a close.

"Good morning, Deputy Chief Officer," Peggy spoke up from a corner, behind the open door.

"Ah, yes. Mrs. Pinch, I am pleased to see you." There was sufficient hesitation in the gruff voice for everyone to doubt the sentiment. "The Chief Constable has asked me to ensure that you have every assistance." He spoke without looking at her.

"Mr Wistow, here, represents the War Office," Peggy said.

The policeman snorted.

"It is a broadly interpreted role," Wistow explained. "A retained post."

Peggy felt out of place. With important men in the room, ready to do business, she had no further role in the discussion. With not quite a bob, she slipped out of the room.

The Deputy Chief Officer dropped to an uncomfortable wooden chair, normally in place for suspects. He was bothered by the threadbare carpet. On his previous visit to the station, a similar carpet had covered the cobblestones in the disused stable and he wondered if it had been removed to the inspector's floor as some measure of disrespect.

"Please, tell me if I have got this wrong," he said, bringing his thoughts to order. "Her statement is enough to arrest Templar but not enough to hold him. Our witness is unreliable and embellished her answers with detail which she thought we wanted to hear. Of course, it may be that the kernel of her evidence is good stuff. Templar may have murdered this woman." He reached for the pocket book on the edge of Wistow's desk. "Yes, this Police Constable Evans. Let's have him in. And please, a message to your desk sergeant. He's to stop this 'Aye Aye' malarkey."

Hawk had arrived with the official Bible. "I'm afraid the inspector has gone shopping, sir."

"Yes, yes, yes."

A young constable stepped forward. "I'm Evans."

"Constable Evans, you were here all the time. You noted down the witness's answers? You were in the room? Who told you to do that?"

"No one, sir. I was standing at the door. Sort of a sentry, I suppose."

"Yes, well. Your sergeant will issue a new notebook and this old one is no longer your concern. You may go. Now, where is the bleeding woman?"

Peggy was giving the cutlery and crockery their first proper wash of the week. Then, given time, she would start on the cooker and - 'oh my God' - the painted cupboards. The tea room was a cubby hole for the common man and she expected to be disgusted when she got to the waste tin. She had already taken down the photograph of the Deputy Chief which had hung on the wall as a convenient target for chewed paper pellets. The picture, with hazy margins, showed his younger days when he wore a black tie squeezed to a tiny knot and a moustache trimmed to little more than stubble. The photograph had been taken by Windsors who, in those days, had been situated next door to Templar Simms and Harcourt before a scandal caused their closure.

"If you please, miss," said the young policeman at the door. "It's our Deputy Chief Officer. He's issuing orders left, right and centre. He's already put Sergeant Hawk in his place and I've had a wigging for doing my job properly. He wants to see you."

"Does he now?" she asked without slowing down.

"Yes, miss. Sort of, demands to see you."

"I am a married woman," said Peggy, not in her best mood, "which makes me Mrs. Pinch or madam."

"Yes, ma'am. The Deputy Chief, ma'am"

"And who is to do this cleaning?"

"I suppose, ma'am, it can wait until the Deputy Chief has finished with you."

Peggy screwed up a tea towel and threw it to the draining board. "Very likely it will, young man."

By now, the Deputy was behind the inspector's desk and Wistow was in the suspect's chair. He stood up as Peggy walked into the office and helped her to the seat. Sergeant Hawk hovered.

"Stand up, Mrs. Pinch. Here, take the Bible in your right hand and hold it up." The Deputy Chief knew the oath by heart. "Repeat, I solemnly swear that I shall serve the King in the office of constable …"

And so, in less than sixty seconds, Peggy Pinch was enrolled in the Borough Police as a Temporary Detective Officer. The circumstance was unusual and necessitated some discussion regarding the placement of the word 'woman'. Should it come after the 'temporary' or between the 'detective' and 'officer.'

"A matron will be called in to instruct you regarding your hair and how to walk before we let you loose on the streets," he advised. "Are you proud?"

"Yes, sir."

"And so you should be."

She wondered if she should salute. Instead, she bobbed and the old fool glowed.

"Sit down. The important thing is that you now do as you are told. Specifically, you do only what I tell you to do. No freelancing. No digging up murderers in your back garden. Understand? I know you do."

Wistow was beaming. He wanted to congratulate her but thought twice about fracturing force protocol.

"Is this man Templar a traitor?"

"We're not sure," the farmer replied. "He has been investigated by 5b on two occasions and was given a clean bill of health. His name crops up too often in uncomfortable places. But your investigation must take precedence. He'd get fifteen years for treason but he'll hang for murder."

"All the same, you would prefer me not to arrest him?"

"We always prefer the long game. I'd like to see him run. He'd have to show his hand eventually."

"You've looked at our case?"

"Your sergeant has done well. He called for any relevant sightings."

The Dep was already fingering more than thirty message receipts.

"The response has been very creditable," said Wistow. "Most creditable, given how little time we've had. Two relevant leads have emerged. The first, a parcel of the correct size was dispatched from the Market Square Post Office, the morning after the murder. Unfortunately, we have no description of the sender."

"It was a man," Peggy put in.

"Indeed," said Wistow.

"To what address?"asked the Dep.

"Unnoticed, unfortunately. But Tanganyika. It could be several weeks before we are able to trace it, if at all."

The Deputy muttered, "Devil's tooth," and Peggy said quietly, "A red herring," then put her fingers to her lips.

"I mean, meant to delay us." She nodded and, the Deputy made a fist of his left hand and smacked it repeatedly.

"Now come on, man. Let's have some progress. That pile of sightings must have produced something better than soggy apple pie being posted to East Africa."

"The morning after the murder ..."

The Deputy Chief's ears pricked up.

"A woman, of whom we have a detailed description, deposited a sealed wooden box in our local bank."

"That's the stuff!"

Thirty minutes later, Peggy was perched on a milking stool at the foot of the police stairs. She was having her hair pinned by a big-bosomed matron who wore two chevrons on her unbuttoned tunic and spoke with the smouldering stub of a dry looking cigar in her mouth. "Always wear it up and make sure nothing grows within half an inch of your collar. You are all right, here, with plenty of room. No stray tails and no fringe, of course. I can see that you don't wear a fringe; usually, I have trouble only with the younger women. Although you are not in uniform, you must walk in step. You'll find that the men prefer to walk slowly; they plod. To get there too late to do anything is clever policing. Remember, a good policeman gets neither wet nor out of breath and, ladylike, can be neither shocked nor surprised. Now, what has he done to you? Temporary Detective Officer. Not a Special Constable? Mind, our Deputy Chief Officer likes to invent new ranks. He thought that our men were a slovenly lot, so he

147

appointed a Police Sergeant Major. Only two other forces have such a thing. There are plenty of matrons, but the Dep wanted to have one of his own type, so he made me an Under Sergeant Major. My goodness, the men don't like it. Don't get promoted, my dear.

Peggy asked, "Who said 'Wheeler is willing,' ?"

"No-one. But Barkis said 'Barkis is willing'. It's from *David Copperfield*." Without a pause, she continued, "Of course, he is quite mad. You do know that, don't you? He was two weeks in an asylum before they said that he wasn't mentally ill. They actually gave him a paper saying that he wasn't mad. Well, there can be no better evidence of madness than that! Don't worry too much about the rules, if you are here for only one case. You know what I think about your murder? I walked through your village the morning after it was done and do you know who I think done it? Why, the girl at the vicarage."

Although she knew that Matron's suspicion was no more that playful, Peggy explained,. "She was at the wrong end. The murderer approached along a path we call the Waddie so he came from lower down the village. That's what I think, anyway."

"I saw her in the Rector's front garden and she was plucking. I say, never trust a woman who plucks flowers when she could just as well pick."

Peggy's reply confounded the matron.

"I can see that is forceful evidence. Most forceful when applied to someone else. You see, the vicar's maid becomes important when she's a go-between for two others. An innocent or deliberate accomplice? I've yet to make up my mind."

Matron thought she had been talking nonsense. Her face twisted, screwed up then went wide eyed: "Money. The oldest and best motive. Always look for the money." But she withdrew to a sheepish look, repeating under her breath, 'Never trust a woman who plucks flowers' .

Chapter Thirteen
Wistow Conducts Enquiries

Peggy had not walked through the tall doors of a bank before. Policemen were paid in cash, sent postal orders through the post and kept their savings under the bed. The Great War emphasised that saving with the Post Office was patriotic but, said Arthur Pinch, his patriotism did not stretch to letting Mary at the village Post Office know how much money he had.

She had expected the hall to be warm, comfortable and welcoming, but the coal fire in the lobby was frugal and the quiet was intimidating. Even those sounds which were natural and everyday in a commercial office - the ting of a typewriter's bell, telephone calls and buzzers on desks - seemed dampened and muffled, and no one seemed to fuss with them.

No one welcomed them. While Wistow was recognised within moments and taken off to the bank manager's office, Peggy stepped quietly to an isolated chair against a wall and sat down. She had not thought before that silence might have an echo. Or that crossing her ankles could make enough noise to lift an enquiring look from a bespectacled cashier. This twiddling of her thumbs was interrupted when Billy Wheeler emerged through a maple wood door that protected the barricade.

"My chief cashier has allowed me ten minutes," he explained as he ushered her into a cupboard room close to the double doors. She sat, he stood and they could hear pedestrians on the pavement outside.

"Is Miss Nevers having a baby?" he asked directly.

"Well, goodness. I mean, it's hardly my place to say. You know me, Billy, I'm not one to spread talk. Gosh, you know how to flummox a lady. I don't know which way to look."

"But Miss Nevers is?"

Peggy pursed her lips and nodded once. "Definitely. No one has any doubt."

"Then, I need to marry her." He sighed, as if the prospect was not entirely welcome. "You know my situation. Audrey has walked out on me. I've no idea where she is but she plainly means our Tom to be my responsibility."

"He is your son," Peggy reminded him.

Wheeler stayed quiet.

"I can't say that I'll enjoy the gossip," he said, his eyes on the bare light bulb in the middle of the ceiling.

"Oh, come now. Country girls have always found this way up the aisle. It may be sordid in the towns but it is everyday business where you and I live."

"No, you misunderstand. I love Maud and where's the man who wouldn't be proud for such a good woman to carry his child. But, you know that she has money?"

Peggy shook her head.

"Rather a lot actually. She was an only child and the only niece of two dead uncles."

Peggy relaxed her shoulders and crossed her ankles again. "Well, let's you and I list the women who are going to make something of that. And make something they will. Who goes to the top of the list? Mary in the Post Office, Dolly Johnson without a doubt. There's Cart and Gort, though Gort I think not. And not one of them matters."

"You're right, of course. Will you ask her?"

Peggy straightened up. "I most certainly will not! This will be the first proposal she has received and you will do it properly. You will buy a bunch of flowers and go down on one knee." She thought a little. "But Pinch will offer to give her away."

"Mr Wheeler, please!" The call went across the hall like a child experimenting with shouts across a canyon. "The manager's office for Mr Wheeler, please!"

Farmer Wistow had been treated to a cigar of better quality than anything a police matron ever smoked. The sherry and glasses were on the manager's desk top and, curiously, a side plate of red salmon chunks. Wistow, never able to relax until his boot laces were undone and the front tails of his shirt brought out of his waistband, reflected that he had borrowed more money in this room than in any room in England. And, he had offered more explanations why he would not be repaying it on time. "Come now, Featherstone," he liked to tease. "You make your money when I don't pay it back. You write the figures I owe in your books, don't you? And pretend that it's there to be counted. That's how this banking lark works. You count up the money that doesn't exist." He sucked on the cigar. "It makes the Surrey classes thunderously rich."

"I thought you weren't here to talk about your indebtedness and my margins." The bank manager was slightly portly, a little short and too round faced to accommodate the handlebar moustache (trimmed back on the advice of his area manager.) He liked to stand with the thumb of his left hand tucked in his waistcoat jacket.

"That was before you displayed the customary sherry. It's difficult to break a habit." Wistow turned his head as Wheeler knocked and brought Peggy into the room. "Ah, Peggy, Mr Featherstone was about to explain how his bank accepted a valuable parcel for safe-keeping."

Featherstone, showing professional patience with a flamboyant but embarrassing client, asked, "You have the Deposit Book, Mr Wheeler?"

The ledger was opened on the desk and four pairs of eyes searched for the relevant entry.

"You accepted the deposit yourself, Mr Wheeler?"

"No, sir. Mr Jackson served the lady. But you will see that I have countersigned the entry. In view of the customer's excessive valuation, I oversaw the parcels secure dispatch to the central depository, the following day."

"Admirable," Featherstone said. "Now, Mr Wistow, you will see that we have a name and address."

"Good lord." He lifted his face and looked at Peggy. "The parcel was left by the dead woman's sister."

Back in the police station, Peggy Pinch completed the washing up and had made a good start on the cupboard doors before the Deputy Chief Officer walked into the kitchen. "Ah, good. You're still here. That's good. I've solved it."

"Oh, thank heavens."

"No, not the murder. The puzzle you set the lads in the front office. How can somebody be the only child and only niece of two dead uncles? It works with a comma after 'child'. So she has no brothers and sisters, and each of her uncles have no other nieces." He picked up the framed photograph from the table. "Oh, what's this?"

"I am going to give it a bit of a polish. The lads have it on a nail in the wall."

"A portrait of me? On their kitchen wall? Mrs. Pinch, I am touched, truly touched."

The Deputy Chief Officer's self assessment was common talk before tea-time.

Left alone, Peggy was determined to get the grubby marks off the paintwork before the late shift of policemen broke their patrols for refs at tea-time. With less than twenty minutes to go, Sergeant Hawk walked into the kitchen.

"There's a fair bit of talk," he said.

"I'm sure there is," Peggy replied without lifting her eyes from the balding scouring brush.

"Scuttlebuck, most of it."

She said "I suppose scuttlebuck's to be expected," although she wasn't sure what Hawk was talking about.

"I've said."

"Would you like to share a pot of tea, Sergeant Hawk? The kettle's boiled. Only, I am a bit busy with the marks on this paintwork."

"Oh yes. Do you want to finish your cleaning before you put it on?"

"No I do not! I want you to boil some bloody water in the bloody kettle!"

"Oh, of course. Straight away. I'll brew up."

She asked, "You've said what?"

"I beg your pardon."

"You said, I said and I wondered what it was you said."

"Only two people know the truth."

"Ah, you'll be discussing the perils of my rear end."

"Well?"

"Well what? Did I get a pinched bottom from George Templar?" She said, "I can see how that is an important question," and she sat down, inevitably, to play mother.

Chapter Fourteen

Jessica Knightly in Metroland

When Farmer Wistow changed gear and roared through Clophill, Peggy thought of fat Mr Toad racing his motor through the countryside with no thought for others. "What to you think of her!" he guffawed over the row of beating pistons. "She's an American job. A Terraplane. Not another like her in the country."

He slapped the coachwork enthusiastically. "Old Wistow's having his breakfast one morning when a gent from Chicago arrives and says 'Twenty pounds, sir, and you'll store my automobile in one of your old barns until I can fix her shipment back to the States.' What do you think of that?"

Peggy tightened her grip on her seat as he swept through a double bend.

"I'll tell you what Wistow says to himself. My man from Chicago can write all the letters, send all the telegrams and dispatch willowy agents to knock on my door but as long as old Farmer Wistow does nothing, he gets to keep this fine fiery monster." He laughed, blasting the horn and snaking from one side of the road to the other. "You better tell your husband, Mrs. Pinch, that he has a car thief in his parish!"

Fifteen minutes later, the couple were sitting in long grass within the sound of a churning watermill. Peggy lifted some muslin cloth from the tops of two picnic baskets while Mr

Wistow uncorked a flagon of cider and poured it into wooden beakers for each of them.

"Here, chicken and mustard," he beamed as he opened a serviette. "Slips down a treat, it does, with farmyard cider and a hunk of cheese."

"Your car looks splendid in the sunshine," she promised. "But I won't be sharing her credentials in our police house."

"You're easy on the eye, Mrs. Pinch; I've always said so."

"You just mind your tongue, Horace Wistow. I'll hear nothing from you that wouldn't be said in front of my husband."

"You're going to hear some truths, this afternoon, and I'm not sure how to prepare you. People serve their country in different ways, remember that, and sometimes those ways cannot avoid intrigue."

Peggy said, "There is one question yet to be answered. I can't see how it's important and it's probably not. But I don't like questions that cannot be answered."

She got to her feet and took half a dozen steps away from him. She looked across the fields as she tried to solve her puzzle. When he joined her, she explained, "Jamie Eider said that Polly Adam had told him that I wanted to see him." She shook her head. "That's simply not possible. I rang his mother from the phone in the vicarage lobby. Polly couldn't have heard me because she was standing on the terrace. The door to the Ladies Parlour was open and I could see Polly through the French windows. She couldn't have heard me. At first, I thought that June on the switchboard had been listening in, but that wouldn't explain how Polly knew what I was saying. Don't you see, there's only one explanation. Someone else must have been in the vicarage. He overheard the conversation and told Polly about it."

"I don't see how that helps. Eliza Knightly was stone cold by that time."

She sighed, "You're right of course. But I don't like things that don't fit."

This was Metroland where, the Underground said, a family man could master a small house and large garden. Each morning, they caught the Metropolitan line to their office work in the city; each evening, they manicured their front hedges. "It's not the countryside that we know," Peggy remarked. "It's false."

"Do you think we'll all be like this one day. Everyone will be in one huge middle class, and old Farmer Wistow won't be spoken of."

Sensing Peggy's curiosity, he took a round about route to Miss Knightly's address. Half the houses were semi-detached. Here, Peggy understood, people read *Popular Gardening, Practical Householder* and *The Passing Show* magazines that stuck on the shelf of her local Post Office. The posher houses were mock Tudor or mock Gothic with, Peggy noticed, mock tiles. Wistow had to park the Beast on the open because 'Boelyn Eaves' had neither a driveway nor a garage. By the time they had disembarked - and disembarking was how it felt - Miss Knightly had come to her front gate to welcome them.

"Well, Orrice, you old blackguard, you old spy," she called as she led through the elaborate porch, with a bench that no one had sat upon, and into a living room that extended the length of the ground floor. There was an extra armchair, two tables instead of one, and two standard lamps (one overlooking an armchair, the other in the far corner.) "I know what you are thinking," she said. "Hot and cold running water, electric light, floors that don't flood and wonderful wireless reception. Well, you try finding a competent maid, a reliable cleaning lady and, God bless 'em, window cleaners that know how to do the job."

Peggy was quiet. She had been in posh houses before but they had been owned by posh people. Here, Miss Knightly was like her departed sister and Peggy and Arthur Pinch, but she had got on in ways that poor Eliza and the Pinches had not. For the first time, she was embarrassed by the way that she and Arthur lived, without ambition, in the rent free police house.

"Darling, do sit down. Horace is more comfortable on his feet when he drinks tea." She leaned forward in her armchair. "He tends to slop. Now, you, Peggy, tell me how you found the spy in our midst?"

Peggy had stayed on her feet. She suggested uncertainly, "I've more than an idea who it is, but I've not enough to bring them to court."

Knightly put two Bourbon Creams on the side of a saucer and handed the cuppa across the low table. "Oh, don't worry. We'll soon turn them, and they'll be working against these Germans rather than for 'em."

"He's run off."

"Then you're talking of Sir Roland. How did you first suspect him?"

"Old fashioned detective work, I'm afraid. Laborious and pains-taking. I went through the letters and noted the dates when Eliza's soldier thought the spycatchers were onto him. The most important letter was missing."

"Yes and when do you think that was stolen?"

"Immediately after the murder. I supposed Mr Wistow took it. As evidence, it was too important to your office to leave lying around. He took it into custody."

Miss Knightly smiled, Farmer Wistow went 'umph' and produced the letter from his jacket pocket.

"It's all right. Really, it makes no difference. I checked the dates against the days when little Sir Roland was home from school."

"How on earth ... ?

"I cross referenced them with the Country Beat Occurrence Book and the wordy journal of one of our old vicars."

"After all these years ... ?"

"Neither the diocese nor the constabulary are enthusiastic weeders, and the aged rector suspected that Sir Roland was building a wireless transmitter, suspicions he shared with the village constable. The had no real evidence, nothing that would have justified a search warrant. But they did keep a note of Sir Roland's comings and goings. But when the grown-up Sir Roland thought that I was on to him - which I wasn't, at that stage - he attacked me in the vicarage. We knocked him out, I'm afraid. I ran to the telephone at the bottom of the vicar's stairs but by the time Arthur got there, Sir Roland had recovered and ran off."

She sensed that Wistow was trying to catch her eye. They made faces at each other before Peggy's attention settled on the corner of the sideboard. She wasn't sure, at first, so moved closer in little half steps. There, between an ashtray and a little tin of Songster gramophone needles was a single cigarette card.

Miss Knightly was saying, "He'll show his face, sooner or later. I have learned, darling, that spies are not very good at their jobs. The traits that make spies also make bad spies. Another cup?" She asked, as she poured, "Are you any closer to identifying who deposited the church treasure in my name?"

"The description fits you," said Peggy. There, in plain sight, was faggy card Number Twenty One.

"I'm afraid not," the lady laughed.

"The description was quite detailed," said Wistow.

"I promise you, arresting me won't help. I have lain some bait. Three quarters of an inch in the Deaths Column, although the incompetent clerk couldn't get it right. He preferred to spell morning without the 'u'. Morning dress. His readers probably thought he was inviting them to a wedding."

Peggy's face froze. She felt her ankle was going to give way. She stammered, "I --I can't, yes" She held out a hand to steady herself against the back of the chair.

"I need to telephone, straight away."

The others followed her to the pedestal in the lobby. She told the operator, "I need to phone my Police Station at home. It's long distance. "

"Yes, madam. You mean that you need a trunk call. What time would you like to book?"

"Now. I must phone now."

"We can try, madam, but I cannot promise a connection."

Wistow: "Phone the local station here, Peg. They'll put it through."

Knightly: "My office. Tell my office and they'll express it."

Then Peggy's local operator came on the line. "I am sure that he's at home, Peggy. He's just been speaking to Sergeant Hawk about arrangements for his retirement. He mentioned the Watch Committee but I couldn't really follow. Let me try his number."

Peggy put a hand over the mouthpiece. "It's June. She's usually very good. We have her round for tea."

Arthur Pinch, who was far from fluent on the telephone, was standing in full uniform with his trousers and underpants around his thighs. "Yes, Policeman Pinch speaking. Who's there?"

"Catch the vicar's maid, Arthur! Arrest Polly Adam!"

Chapter Fifteen
The Case of the Cuddly Kitten

The boys from the bordering borough were back and worried that they were beaten. Between them, they had experienced less than a handful of murderers like this. Murderers, not by circumstance or opportunity but by diligent malice aforethought. Their suspect had known what questions she would be asked and she had built them into her plans so that she didn't need to come up with answers. The longer the detectives spent with her, the more the evidence provided answers in her favour.

"You can't charge me with the murder of Roland Byrivers because you haven't a body. You can't have murder without a body. The coroner cannot even sit on a case until the man's been gone for more than seven years."

"Bunkum."

"Charge me."

The fat one said, "Oh, we'll charge you, never mind the evidence. They can hang you only once, Polly. They'll do it at eight o'clock on a Thursday morning in the bowels of Wandsworth gaol. You'll have spent the last night with a wardress. (We wouldn't want you to harm yourself before the hangman gets his chance.) They usually play draughts with their condemned prisoner or have a go at a complicated jigsaw. Gin Lane is a favourite choice, so they say. They keep it in the chaplain's cupboard, especially for the occasion."

The young one, leaning against the window ledge and looking as if he hadn't moved since their last visit, asked, "Once we've got that far, I've often wondered what it's like to be left praying for a last minute reprieve. What do you think, will you be one of those?"

"If you get that far," mocked Polly.

"Then, at two minutes to eight, the warder will fill the kettle from the last flagon of water and put it on the tiny camping stove, knowing that it won't boil before they've done with you. Warders are cruel like that. A good hanging takes less than twenty seconds. The prison governor will lead the chaplain and the hangman into your cell. The priest might be reciting a prayer, or he may wait until they've bound your arms to your body and put the black hood over your head. How are you feeling, Polly?"

She didn't answer. She hadn't pictured this before. "How do you know that she wasn't dead before the intruder injected the poison?"

"Is that your defence?"

"I don't need to defend anything. You have to prove it."

"Not really. You see, you are the confident sort. You're cocky and the jury won't like you. They'll listen to the prosecuting counsel, take one look at you and you'll be as good as hung. You come across as wicked and no amount of clever planning can change that."

She said, "Your blood test doesn't prove it. It doesn't show that the poison was injected before or after she died."

The fat one was sufficiently long in the tooth that he avoided any comment which he couldn't be sure of. He continued, "Hooded, and bound so tightly that your body's twisted just a little, they'll guide you to that door that you've not been looking at, all through the night. Still, the kettle isn't boiling. They'll push you forward. You'll have time to say, for a last time, 'I didn't do it,' as they strap your ankles and before the trapdoor opens. The chief engineer is waiting below and he'll catch your legs so that an extra tug makes sure your neck's broken and you've gone."

"They're not supposed to do that," smiled the younger detective. "It might be against the law but, you know, a dead man's never tested the case."

"If you don't fancy it, mess yourself on the way down. The chiefs are less keen then." He paused before concluding, "The evidence is nothing to do with it. It's all because the jury won't like you, Polly Adam."

With a glance and a nod to each other, the detectives adjourned to the refs room.

The doctor, Wistow and the Deputy Chief Officer were standing in the inspector's office, leaning, perching, changing positions, flexing and stretching. Peggy was sitting in a leather chair, brought in for the purpose. She had one knee crossed over the other and promised herself that she would keep quiet.

"I am sorry, gentlemen," Meriweather was saying, "but our knowledge is incomplete. The poison was neither ingested nor inhaled so the usual tests don't apply. We could look at the colour of the blood but that is notoriously unreliable and as likely to mislead in one direction as another. There are some more delicate measures. Some people say that testing the hair or fingernails will show whether the poison was delivered ante or post mortem, but specialist witnesses will readily point out that hair and fingernails continue to grow after death. What's more, the victim may be dead but the poison may still be alive; it might continue to react with the tissue. I wouldn't like to go to court with it. The point, unfortunately, is that evidence of this nature will always provoke legitimate argument and offer an element of doubt." He added unnecessarily, "A quite reasonable doubt."

Wistow asked, "What about a murder case without a body?"

"Captain Kidd wasn't so lucky," said the Deputy Chief Officer. "No, it's not law but persuading a jury is notoriously difficult."

"There would be no medical evidence of the cause of death," remarked the doctor

"And the risk of a miscarriage of justice would hang over the whole trial," said the Deputy Chief. "No, we'd never prove that Sir Roland is dead. She's right about that. The body was left alone in an upstairs study. Only four people were in the house and when Constable Pinch got to the locked room, the body had gone. The immediate conclusion would never be that the corpse was removed and cleverly hidden in just a few minutes. No, the weight of circumstantial evidence would lend to the view that he debunked through the window." He added, "I think he probably did."

"Oh, follow the evidence!" exclaimed a frustrated Peggy. She had heard enough debate. When the two detectives walked into the room, suitably watered, rested and ready to go again, she addressed them directly. "Let me speak with her."

The fat one shook his head. "You're too much involved. You're part of the investigation. The defence would claim that your evidence is prejudiced."

"Who the devil are you!" barked the Deputy. "Do I know you!"

"Sergeant Courtney and Constable Davies from the force next door, sir"

"Are you any good?"

"Not really, sir."

"Then thank God for that!"

The Deputy Chief turned his back on the company and looked out the window. Others kept quiet; in spite of his discourtesy, it would still have been bad manners to talk to a superior's back. He said, without looking at them, "Mrs. Pinch is essentially a witness. We can confront the suspect with her evidence, quite reasonably. I agree with you, Sergeant Courtney, it would be unusual for her to lead with questions. The court might make something of that, who knows?" He nodded, and shrugged as he turned around. "Give your evidence in the form of a verbal statement, Mrs. Pinch. Adams," (he got her name wrong throughout the enquiry) "may take or leave her opportunity to respond."

The air was heavy with dissent from the boys of the borough, but they said nothing.

He asked Peggy directly, "How sure are you of your ground?"

"She killed Eliza Knightly. No other explanation fits the facts."

He grunted, glanced at the two detectives, looked at Wistow and the doctor and raised an enquiring eyebrow. "Then I am ready to charge her, however it goes."

When they brought her out to an exercise yard, surrounded by the brick walls of the police station, Polly guessed that this was how it felt to be put against a wall and shot.

Peggy stood in the middle of the little square like a heavier boxer commanding a ring.

She said, "Polly, I'll not protect you. You killed an old lady in our village."

The prisoner didn't answer.

"No one will charge you with stealing the church plate. After all, you didn't really steal it, did you? You always intended it to come back to its rightful owner. Banking it in the name of Eliza's sister was very clever. Of course, you knew that she would deny all knowledge and the plate would be free. Asking Reverend Sullivan to post the first parcel was more risky. He could easily have spoken up. I think that was a risk too far, but who am I?"

Peggy looked for the suggestion of a smile, but her adversary was poker faced.

"It made us think that we were after a couple rather than one person, and you got away with it. The murder of Sir Roland? You and I know that you were defending me and, anyway, people are growing less and less convinced that the bastard is dead. I thought I knew, but Pinch is there, drip-drip-dripping more doubt each time we speak of it. You, sure as Hades, know the truth but you're keeping it to yourself. No-one's going to charge you with that."

My God, thought the fat detective, taking notes that he later threw away, she's banking on a confession to the murder in the cottage.

"But you were sure that Miss Knightly had seen you break into the Hall."

Peggy noticed that Polly Adam had to stop herself from shaking her head.

"Oh, I see. You were only exploring that night. You took the church plate on the night of the murder. That was very brave of you, Polly. Good Lord, Pinch was putting himself about everywhere."

This time, there was no reaction.

The fat detective, watching from a first floor window, was bubbling with frustration. Mrs. Pinch was playing her best cards, one by one, and getting nowhere. She was giving their game away.

"Nevertheless, exploration or otherwise, she had seen you and needed to be put out of the way. But, you couldn't think that was a right thing to do. You're not a wicked person, Polly? You have a conscience about these things."

The suspect opened her mouth to speak. She hesitated and, for the first time, the trace of tears appeared in her eyes. She had been walking around the yard making Peggy, in the middle, twirl to keep her in view. Now, she went to the corner of a wall. "I've nothing to say."

"But then you remembered the newspaper clipping from 1916 and the old vicar's note that people in the village suspected Miss Knightly of giving information to the Germans. If she had betrayed her country, if she was a traitor, then perhaps murder was excusable."

"Peggy ..."

"It's always been difficult for you, hasn't it. Your shoulder and your neck. I suppose people say you've a cock-eyed look about you. And if I turn way from you, like this, you cannot pick up what I am saying." Peggy smiled at her. "Because you have to watch our lips, don't you? Even now when you don't want to hear what I've got to say, you need only walk behind me. How well can you lip read, Polly? When you stood on the terrace, you understood what I was saying on the vicar's phone. Did you pick out what Farmer Wistow and Eliza were saying when you were exploring the Twitchels? Oh, you certainly worked out what Dolly Johnson was shouting at Miss Knightly in her back garden because you mentioned it to Little Thin Annie. Polly, it seemed to you that everyone knew that Miss Knightly was a traitor. Perhaps, they would thank you for finishing her off."

"I don't want you to say any more. I don't have to listen."

"Let's move on. Sullivan was out of the way that afternoon; no-one would know that you were absent from the vicarage. Did you go to Jamie Eider for the poison? No, you didn't need to. Crushed mothballs - they needed to be out of date - were easily found in the dusty vicarage. So, now, we move on to the cats. Polly, nothing to do with the cats was necessary. This was where you let your nasty side get the better of you."

Peggy took a step towards her. "Why did Miss Knightly think that Queen O'Scots was staring at her?"

When the suspect stayed quiet, Peggy warned, "Polly, I've said that I'll not protect you. You killed an old lady in our village."

Still, she didn't answer.

"Right. Well, we know the answer to the first question. Because Queenie was the only black cat she knew. Do you have other black cats in the vicarage?"

Polly Adam shook her head.

"We know the answer to that question. Yes, there is a litter in the rectory paddock. Why did you put poison on the black cat's claw?"

"Peggy you're going too fast," she pleaded. "Let me answer."

"But we know the answers, Polly. You wanted the black cat to poison things so that people would worry about a witch's familiar. It was your murder and you wanted it tinged with the macabre, the Mark of Cain, and black cats that do a witch's evil for her. Now, the question which I want to hear you answer. We all know the truth, but I would like you - the woman who came to our sleepy village and used an old myth to steal from our church and an old woman's superstition to do murder - I want to hear you say it."

"No, Peggy." Polly Adam tilted her head back. Her eyes brimmed with tears.

"Why wouldn't the cat scratch the old woman?"

At last, she spoke out. "Oh, because she liked her. Can you believe that? I'd brought her up to be a witch's familiar and then she wanted to curl up on the target's lap."

"What did you do to her?"

"I injected her myself."

"In the end, yes. But not at first, Polly, you didn't. You rubbed in Miss Reynold's mustard to soften the skin, then you took the poisoned paw and scratched and scratched and scratched."

She buried her head in her hands and blurted. "You don't know that! You can't say it in court!"

"Polly, I don't want to say it in court but I do want you to tell me. What did you do to the cat?"

"She had to be extinguished. Like some horrid charcoal drawing on the coal house wall, she had to be wiped away."

Peggy asked again, "What did you do with the cat?"

"I ought to have burned her alive but I couldn't get it right. So I drowned her first."

"You held her head under the water?"

Polly Adam nodded. "Then I soaked her body in petrol and set fire to her."

"Was this before or after she was dead."

The murderer shook her head. "I hate you, Peggy Pinch."

Chapter Sixteen

Parlour Talk

Moments when Peggy Pinch was required to act like a grown up usually produced a queasiness in her tum. She reacted with the fidgets which soon became a thirst for snapping at people without thinking first. But the vicarage made a difference. That afternoon, she worked merrily in the kitchen, 'pom-poming' and 'la-la-ing' to herself as she visited every corner of the clerical larder. She made Pinch a cup of tea at three, put out some scraps for the waifs and strays that prowled the village and, by four o'clock had prepared an afternoon tea for ten which she laid in the ladies sitting room, overlooking the vicarage garden. The evening promised to be cool with a clear sky, so she left the way open to the terrace. Light from the parlour lay a beam across the paving, the low stone wall and down three steps to the long untendered grass.

Farmer Wistow arrived first and smoked a cigar beyond the French windows, repeatedly patting the stone carved jockey on his head. The two from Templars came next; they too waited on the patio. Dr Meriweather came in with Bill Wheeler, while Dolly Johnson waited at in Vicarage Lane until Pinch was ready to escort her inside. Mrs Templar thought it better not to come. Dr Knightly from Metroland thought she was last but, no, Reverend Sullivan arrived some minutes later having completed a pastoral visit to a couple in Back Lane.

When the ladies were seated and the gentlemen had found suitable corners or props to stand against, Peggy began with concern for the vicar.

"How is the remembering going?" she asked.

"Very nicely, thanks to Doctor Meriweather. I am under his medication. We have a fine practitioner."

The doctor insisted, "But a thorough rest is what you really need, my boy. I've had a word with your bishop and you are off to a retreat for three weeks. We will all be here when you get back."

"Yes." He was nodding and locking his fingers in some strange knot. "Yes, yes. And the church plate too. Back where it belongs. But how did she know that the plate was secure in Sir Roland's safe?" questioned the vicar.

Wistow answered. "She didn't, for sure. But, given that one brother of Byriver Hall had accused another of the original theft ..."

"And as good as played out a deadly duel in the old offices of Templar, Simms and Harcourt," put in the solicitor's mistress.

"... the family safe seemed a good place to start."

"But I had no idea," pleaded the vicar, looking around for support. "Not the faintest notion."

"Polly needed to know if anyone in the Twitchels would see her gaining entry by the wrought iron steps to Sir Roland's house. The night before the murder, she walked to the old hedgewatcher's den; she convinced herself that her breaking and entering would be unseen. But she was shocked to catch sight of Miss Knightly at the junction of Back Lane."

Pinch collected a salted wafer from the table, allowed himself a spoonful of mustard, and explained, "This was her night-time walk in carpet slippers. Following the murder, the gamekeeper and I were able to retrace the footprints."

"Eliza, it was her idea we should meet in secret," Farmer Wistow insisted. "She told me that the letter of 25 August was the important one. This gave the clue to the betrayal during the war."

The vicar nodded gravely. "So our Polly saw only two choices. To forego the chance of retrieving the plate or making sure that Eliza Knightly would not talk. Why or why wouldn't she speak with me? But I can answer that myself; I put aside no time for her."

"The next day, she knew that you would be out of the house for the whole afternoon so her own absence wouldn't be noticed. First, she telephoned Templars and, pretending to be Miss Knightly, cancelled their appointment at Wayback Cottage."

"I shouldn't have been so easily fooled," conceded Miss Twinn. "I should have asked more questions."

The doctor concluded, "Adam slipped into Miss Knightly's parlour and while the poor old woman dozed, she injected the poison."

"And in the middle of that night, she burgled Sir Roland's place and removed the stolen church plate," supposed the solicitor. "I can see it now."

"But what to do with it?" piped up Bill Wheeler, whose tea plate had been kept constantly busy. "She couldn't present it to the vicarage without bringing suspicion onto herself."

"That's where she was really very clever," sighed the doctor.

"Very, indeed," said Farmer Wistow.

"Really clever" Peggy agreed.

Constable Pinch explained. "She made up two parcels, one containing the treasure while a second contained the decoy. She asked Sullivan, here, to post the decoy to far off Africa, knowing that it wouldn't be traced for several weeks, if at all. But the genuine parcel, she lodged with Bill's bank under the name of doctor Jessica Knightly."

"The disguise was really very good," Wheeler remarked.

"Very, indeed," said Pinch, taking control of the discussion before the farmer could lodge his two penny worth. "What made you suspect her, Peggy?"

"Well, I didn't until the very last. I had seen the handwritten letters in the Dead Bishops Sittingroom and I had noticed the handwriting on the kitchen 'remind-me', but I didn't connect the two. I needed an extra push, and that was Dr Knightly's mention of her local newspaper misspelling mourning for morning. I remembered that Polly had written Tuesday morning on the kitchen wall. But she had to mean mourning. It seems that it was important for Polly to feel everything she did was justified or, at least, forgiveable."

The vicar understood. He was nodding as he said, "People can confuse the two. They think that if something is forgiveable, then it is excusable."

Miss Twinn caught the relevance. "Peggy's right. Polly didn't mean 'morning.' Peggy saw me coming out of the church on Tuesday afternoon."

Peggy continued. "I think it was Polly's one weakness in this affair. She needed to convince herself that killing Eliza Knightly was not just convenient but it was a right thing to do. She had read the notes in the old journals and she had heard - or, at least, lip read Dolly's accusation that everyone thought she was a traitor - and that became her justification. But I couldn't follow that reasoning until I was sure that Polly had searched the old books. I needed to recognise the writing on the memo board as the writing in the hidden letter. That was the nudge which 'mourning' gave me. Polly meant to make her peace with the Almighty on that Tuesday. I was watching the church as I walked up the Waddie with Dolly. I saw not Polly Adam but Miss Twinn."

"Yes, yes," the vicar said smartly. Then, realising he was about to break a confidence, he kept quiet.

Miss Twinn was downcast. "I had spoken to Mr Sullivan. I couldn't forgive myself for what I had done to poor Lettice and he suggested that I should spend a few quite moments with the Lord, that afternoon."

"That's why I noticed Polly retreating to the vicarage. She needed to postpone her own prayers when she saw you in the pews. And with Dr Knightly's mention of handwriting, it fell into place. All in one go. I was quite surprised how quickly, and how simple it seemed."

"But what," said Farmer Wistow, wading through a mouthful of cheese. "But what on earth had become of Sir Roland?"

"A dreadful accident," Pinch said smartly.

"He surprised me in the Dead Bishop's Sitting-room," said Peggy, determined that no one would learn that she had nearly been ravished. "I thought he was a villain of some sort and Polly bashed him over the head."

"Bashed him?" queried the vicar.

"I thought she'd done for him, truly I did. I called Arthur for help and …"

"... By the time I arrived, the fellow had recovered and had it on his toes."

"Pinch is right. There's no police business there," said Dr Meriwether, reflecting similar comments at the start of the case.

There was a long tail to the evening. Police enquiries were not only complete but fully explained. Each player in the room was allowed a personal smugness that they had suspected parts of the solution all along. Peggy and Pinch felt a professional satisfaction in closing down the elements which, they felt, were better left untouched. Later, Pinch referred to this feeling as his wife's comeliness.

When folk began to leave, Wistow, having feasted sufficiently, drew Peggy Pinch to one corner. Without a word, he withdrew something like a ticket from his jacket pocket. He winked and revealed the faggy of the Spider racing car at the Shelsey Walsh hill climb.

"Well, you old rogue. You pinched that from the sideboard in Metroland."

"No rules apply to collecting cigarette cards," he beamed, red-faced, gloriously replete and every inch a yeoman of old England.

It was dark and cold before they got away from the vicarage and the October mist was coming down. Pinch was experiencing a familiar, settled satisfaction which came with a case showing no loose ends. He felt his parish beat returning to its docile nature. Like a hound, back in her place sat on the hearth rug. "It was young Jamie who produced the poison, wasn't it? I should have kept a close eye on him."

"Oh, I shouldn't do that. No, I don't think that would be at all a good idea."

"Well?"

"He has been experimenting with crumbs of mothballs for months, it seems. I've spoken to him about it. As soon as I got back, I went to see him. We can't discourage him, Pinch. God, that would crush the boy. But he needs to be more careful about how much he reveals to his visitors."

"He needs to keep records," said Pinch.

"Yes, Polly Adam probably stole the naphthalene from his amateur pharmacy but she could have just as likely found a stock of old mothballs in the vicarage. God knows what terrors that horrid house hides."

His slow footsteps, undeniably police trained, sounded distinctly on the stretch of cinder pathway. "Least said, soonest mended," he agreed.

Then Pinch said, "Thank you," carefully enunciating.

"Whatever for?"

"Giving me the arrest. You are still a Special Detective Officer. You had no need to."

Peggy stepped on tip-toes and risked a peck on his cheek. "It will go down as another Arthur Pinch murder. And quite right so. We wouldn't have got there without you. I needed your help, didn't I say? I needed your mind, your memories and your stories of the old village. Remember, Six English Villagers."

"Huh, I got that wrong."

"Not nearly as wrong as me. I always thought it was the doctor." She said, "Adam gave herself away in the end. When she said that she hated me, there was something in her eyes. A proper wickedness."

"Something witch-like, you mean?"

As they reached the churchyard wall, Peggy turned to look at the grey menacing shape of the vicar's rambling house. In there, somewhere, a dead body was hiding.

For the folk who lived between the top and bottom of the village, in The Street or Back Lane, and spent their time in the Post Office queue or at the Red Lion's hearth, the mystery expired on that foggy October night in the vicarage parlour.

Polly Adam was hanged at eight o'clock in the morning, six weeks to the day after she had murdered Eliza Knightly. Peggy made sure she was preoccupied with a tray of apple turnovers. It was a recipe that hardly ever worked for her so she gave it special attention. By the time she checked the clock, it was twenty minutes past eight and it was all over.

The Harvest Festival went well. Edna Carstairs had rallied the children from the school-yard who went trawling for the most obscure produce to offer and Mavis Reynolds, who had been coaching the choir behind closed doors for many more weeks than the new vicar realised, made sure that the singers delivered with holy gusto. Jacoby, not much given to church attendance, caught her ear before the service and whispered that she might like to perform one of her 'dances at midnight.' (He had returned to the crest of Back Lane in secret to enjoy several of the displays, each one more enticing than the last.) Sullivan's nerves were obvious; he had spoken to Doctor Meriweather and Pinch about changing his text in the light of events but it was the farmer who convinced him to persevere with the sermon he had been working on since he took up the living. He reminded the congregation that they were offering thanks on St Luke's day.

And from St Luke, Chapter Seventeen, he told the story of ten lepers of whom only one, a Samaritan, returned to offer thanks after his cure. The villagers were spellbound. Their previous vicar would have lectured them on guilt, vengeance and violence, with a determination that they should all share the guilt of poor Polly Adam. Instead, they were asked to be thankful, a simple message of rural contentment. They had heard it before and, thank goodness, they would hear it for many times to come.

"He bore it beautifully," said Mary, the postmistress.

Shaking the vicar's hand in the church porch, Jacoby suggested that the proceeds from the collection might go to the Royal Agricultural Benevolent Institution.

The next Spring, Reverend Sullivan was the only spectator from the village who witnessed Templar's impressive run up Shelsey Walsh in the Spider. He cut a clipping, very small, from the motoring press and pasted in his new vicarage journal. (You could never tell when it might be of interest.)

The main contents of the Dead Bishop's Sittingroom were removed to the diocesan archive. Should anyone try to open the vicarage journal for 25 August 1916, they will be worried by the two pages glued together with dried blood. The archivist decided that the letter, addressed 'to vicarage wives of times to come' and including an anonymous but very rude rhyme about vicarage beards, should be hidden again and chanced to fate.

The bones are where Polly Adam left them and she took that secret to the gallows.